# THE FINAL QUEST

# The Final Quest

Book 3 of the Quester Trilogy

By

W. B. Speir

Progressive Rising Phoenix Press ®

Published 2024 by Progressive Rising Phoenix Press, LLC
www.progressiverisingphoenix.com

ISBN: 978-1-958640-57-9

Printed in the U.S.A.
1st Printing

Front Cover Photos: "Divine Female Warrior Valkyrie in Winged Helmet Standing on a Dark Background" Stock Photo ID: 2188860069 By Kiselev Andrey Valerevich. Images used under license from Shutterstock.com.

Interior Illustration: "Map of the Portals of ANNWYN." By W. B. Speir. Map Background: "Old Vintage Fantasy Map." Stock Illustration ID: 1305908080 By Olha Andreichyn. Image used under license from Shutterstock.com.

Interior Illustration: "Legendary Sword." Stock Vector ID: 1711886083 By omnimoney. Image used under license from Shutterstock.com.

Cover design by William Speir

Book design by William Speir
Visit: http://www.williamspeir.com

*I thought I had been in love several times in my life. I had been engaged three times before I met my beloved. But after some serious introspection, I realized that, while I had been infatuated and in lust a number of times—and hurt, burned, and betrayed in ways I'll only discuss through my books—I had only been in love twice.*

*The first love, "the one who got away," came into my life to put me on a better path than the one I was following at the time. Once that was done, the fates sent us in different directions, never to meet again.*

*Had all that not happened, I would not have been ready when my beloved came into my life like a whirlwind, bringing changes to my life I could scarcely imagine. But I was ready, and what a ride it has been!*

*It was my beloved who gave me the freedom to write full-time during a difficult period in my life, recognizing that I was happiest when I was writing. For this, I am truly grateful, as I am for all of the blessings and joys this wonderful person has brought to my life.*

*Love is the greatest gift a human being can give or receive. It should never be discarded lightly or entered into for the wrong reasons or with the wrong motives. It is life itself, and it is precious.*

*I love all of you. Thank you for coming with me on this amazing journey.*

# Content Warning:

*The Final Quest* is an adult Romantasy novel. The story includes elements that may not be suitable for all readers. In addition to depictions of violence, this story contains scenes of a strong sexual nature. Readers who may be sensitive to these depictions please take note.

# TABLE OF CONTENTS:

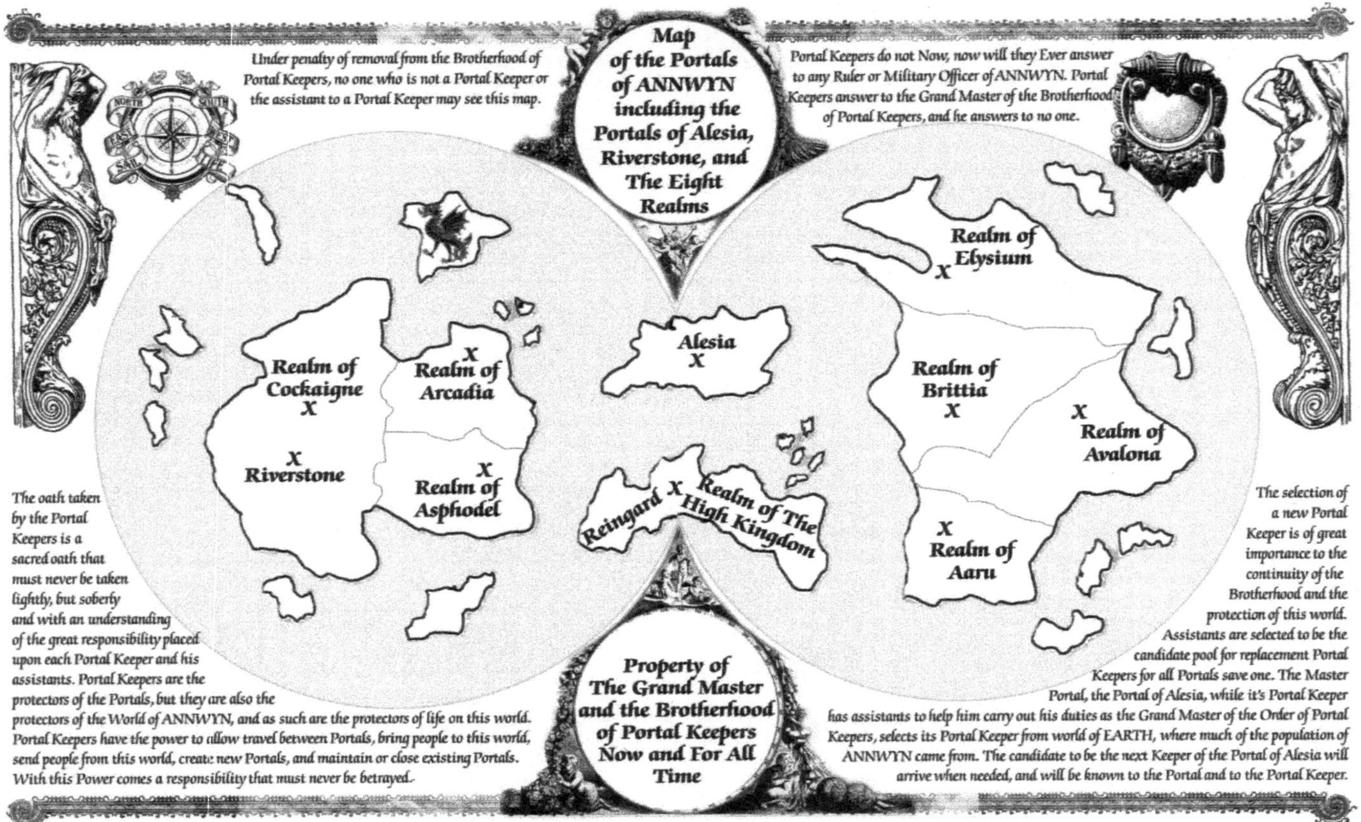
Map of the Portals of ANNWYN including the Portals of Alesia, Riverstone, and The Eight Realms
Under penalty of removal from the Brotherhood of Portal Keepers, no one who is not a Portal Keeper or the assistant to a Portal Keeper may see this map.
Portal Keepers do not Now, now will they Ever answer to any Ruler or Military Officer of ANNWYN. Portal Keepers answer to the Grand Master of the Brotherhood of Portal Keepers, and he answers to no one.
Realm of Cockaigne X
X Riverstone
X Realm of Arcadia
X Realm of Asphodel
Alesia X
Reingard X Realm of The High Kingdom
X Realm of Elysium
Realm of Brittia X
X Realm of Avalona
X Realm of Aaru
The oath taken by the Portal Keepers is a sacred oath that must never be taken lightly, but soberly and with an understanding of the great responsibility placed upon each Portal Keeper and his assistants. Portal Keepers are the protectors of the Portals, but they are also the protectors of the World of ANNWYN, and as such are the protectors of life on this world. Portal Keepers have the power to allow travel between Portals, bring people to this world, send people from this world, create new Portals, and maintain or close existing Portals. With this Power comes a responsibility that must never be betrayed.
Property of The Grand Master and the Brotherhood of Portal Keepers Now and For All Time
The selection of a new Portal Keeper is of great importance to the continuity of the Brotherhood and the protection of this world. Assistants are selected to be the candidate pool for replacement Portal Keepers for all Portals save one. The Master Portal, the Portal of Alesia, while it's Portal Keeper has assistants to help him carry out his duties as the Grand Master of the Order of Portal Keepers, selects its Portal Keeper from world of EARTH, where much of the population of ANNWYN came from. The candidate to be the next Keeper of the Portal of Alesia will arrive when needed, and will be known to the Portal and to the Portal Keeper.

# The Summons

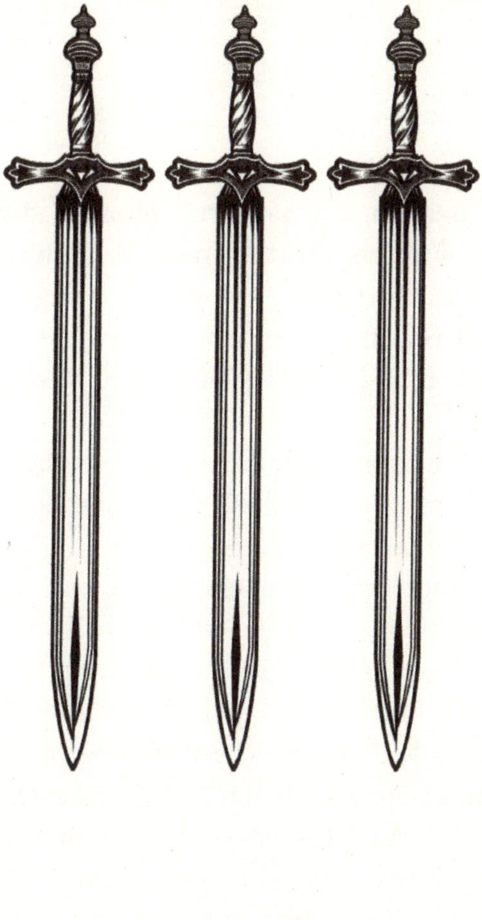

# CHAPTER 1

It had been just over three months since Nichole "Nikki" Frasier, Justin Bradford, Allison Maccabe, Peter Jordan, Olivia "Livvy" Bainbridge, and Kevin Dunross had returned from Annwyn, where they had left Bethany Parrott and Thor Larkin behind to start their new lives together.

And the longer the questers went without accepting any more quests, the less likely it became that they would ever go on another quest again.

Allison and Peter had eloped on one of their long weekend vacations, and they were now living in a house about five blocks from Allison's new hospital. She and a number of the other nurses quit shortly after Bethany did, citing the way Bethany had been treated by management and Human Resources. Allison loved her new hospital, and her schedule allowed her to spend more time at home with Peter, when he wasn't traveling for his clients.

Livvy and Kevin had become true partners—both

personally and professionally. The food service operations that Kevin had asked Livvy to run for him, in the former diner adjacent to his rock-wall climbing center, was doing phenomenally well. Not only was it popular with Kevin's climbers, but it attracted patrons from all over the region, who saw it as an alternative to fast food, cookie-cutter chains, and the expensive trendy spots that opened and then closed at a frightening pace all around the city. The reviews of the restaurant had been glowing, and Livvy loved being the head chef of her own restaurant.

Kevin and Livvy both loved having each other as their life and business partners. They were actively looking for a new place where they could live together, and in the meantime, they alternated between their two apartments, sharing as much time together as they could.

Nikki and Justin were still very much in love and had begun making long-range plans together. Nikki was even looking for a place they could share.

Ever since she had started volunteering with Justin's rock climbing program for veterans with PTSD, Nikki finally had an outlet to give back to her former brothers-in-arms and to help the man who had helped her get over the trauma and impulsive decisions she had made at the end of her army career.

Justin was also helping her get over the memories of the torture she endured the last time they were in Annwyn—one of the reasons Nikki and Justin had both lost interest in taking on any new quests. Nikki still experienced nightmares about what had happened to her, but they mostly occurred on the nights when she and Justin weren't together. She casually mentioned this to him, and he immediately saw to it that they were together every night from that moment on. He was not going to let her keep reliving what had been done to her if there were any way he could help stop it. Nikki was grateful for his willingness to help her get past those intrusive memories. Just his presence alone had such a calming effect on her that she never had nightmares or disturbed sleep when he was there with her.

Both of Nikki's uncles took to Justin immediately, and he was a regular at the gun range where Nikki worked. They both had integrated into each other's lives nicely.

Even though the questers stopped playing games every Saturday night, they still got together often. They were the best of friends, even though what had brought them together originally was no longer a part of their lives.

Nikki discovered that a three-bedroom corner unit was coming available in her building, just down the hall from her current apartment. Between Justin's climbing, jousting, and sword fighting equipment, and Nikki's armor, swords, guns, and RenFaire outfits, an entire bedroom was needed as a storage closet, leaving them a bedroom to share, and a third bedroom for the occasional guests. The price was better than Nikki expected, so she put a hold on the unit until she could show it to Justin.

"I have something to show you," she said when he arrived at her apartment that afternoon.

"We don't have much time," he replied, putting down his gear in her coat closet. He didn't like leaving the expensive climbing gear in his car. "We have to be at the restaurant in an hour."

Nikki smiled. "I'm sure Livvy will hold our table for us. And this won't take that long."

She started walking toward the door, giving Justin a kiss as she passed him.

"Where are you going?" he asked, confused.

"It's just down the hall," she replied.

He followed her out of her apartment and around the corner. Nikki stopped at the last door on the right and unlocked the door.

She turned and grinned. "This apartment just came available, so I had the manager put a hold on it until I could let you see it. You should know that it has three bedrooms, so there's a lot of room for storage. Two of the bedrooms share one of the bathrooms—a Jack-and-Jill configuration. The master bedroom has its own private bathroom. There's also a good sized kitchen and a large living room."

She opened the door and gestured for him to enter. She walked in after him and turned on the lights. Justin immediately began exploring the place, and Nikki followed him, keeping quiet the whole time so she wouldn't say anything that might influence his decision.

As Justin explored the apartment, he checked every closet, mentally pictured his furniture and Nikki's furniture in the space, and checked the location of every electrical and cable outlet. He also spent several minutes in the kitchen, since he did most of the cooking. Nikki helped with the meals, but she was still learning. Justin was the cook between them.

When he was done with all of the other rooms, he stood in the living room space and turned around slowly. When he faced Nikki, he was grinning. "This place is perfect, Nikki! How much is the rent?"

Nikki told him.

Justin's eyes opened wide. "You're kidding! Really? That's what a two-bedroom goes for in my building."

"I'm getting a special rate because I'm a veteran," Nikki confessed, "and because I'm transferring within the same building before my current lease expires. The rent will go up when it renews, but I'll keep my veteran's discount for as long as we live here... if you think this is where you want us to live."

"Anywhere I'm with you is where I want to live," Justin reminded her, "but this place is ideal for us. I say yes. What do you say?"

Nikki threw her arms around his neck and kissed him. "I say, welcome home."

They arrived at the restaurant less than two minutes late, but that didn't stop Livvy from joking that she had to give their table to someone else. Nikki was about to protest when Livvy started laughing.

"I'm kidding, silly. Your usual table is waiting for you. Take a seat, and I'll have someone walk you through today's specials."

Nikki and Justin headed for the corner booth, where they usually ate. The table could hold eight, which was good since Nikki and Justin weren't eating alone that night. Kevin, Peter, and Allison were joining them.

Nikki inhaled deeply as she sat on the circular bench and scooted toward the center. She was enjoying the scents of Livvy's cooking, but a scowl crossed her face, and then she smiled.

"What?" Justin asked. "What's up with that look on your face?"

"I smelled something familiar, and then I realized that I'd smelled it coming from Livvy's apartment the other day. Whatever she's cooking tonight, she practiced it at her place. I didn't get to taste it, but I love the smell."

"Your senses are sharp as ever," Justin commented. "I smell food, but there are too many different aromas coming from the kitchen for me to identify specific dishes."

"And you're the cook in this relationship," Nikki joked.

"Cook, yes. Master Chef, no. The question is, how did you get so good at detecting specific smells?"

Nikki shrugged. "I guess when you've been a soldier as long as I was, the smell of real food is a delicacy that you never take for granted."

Kevin entered the restaurant from the climbing center a minute later, and he joined Nikki and Justin at the table. "Am I too late to hear the specials?" he asked.

Justin shook his head. "I think they're waiting until Allison and Peter arrive."

Kevin pointed toward the door. "Speaking of Peter and Allison, they just got here."

The last two dinner guests walked up to the table and sat down. The diamonds on Allison's engagement and wedding rings caught the light and sparkled with fire.

Before they had time to exchange pleasantries, Livvy's head server appeared at the table to review the day's specials.

When he left with the beverage order, Nikki said, "Livvy's outdoing herself again tonight. No wonder this place is so popular."

Allison glanced at Nikki and caught her eye. "Did you...?" she asked quietly.

Nikki nodded.

"Do what?" Peter asked.

"Show Justin a potential new place for us to live," Nikki said.

"Where?" Kevin asked.

"My building," Nikki answered. "Right around the corner from my place on the same floor. It's a three-bedroom apartment that just came available."

Kevin looked at Justin. "What did you think about it?"

Justin grinned. "It's going to be our new home, as soon as we can sign the paperwork and I can break my current lease."

The others congratulated Justin and Nikki on finding a place.

"Have y'all found a place yet?" Justin asked Kevin.

Kevin blushed. "As a matter of fact..."

Livvy walked up to the table, wearing her white chef's jacket and black chef's skull cap. As she greeted everyone, Nikki saw something glittering on Livvy's finger. Nikki grabbed Livvy's hand and lifted it so she could see it more closely. It was an engagement ring.

Nikki stared at Livvy with her mouth open. "When were you going to tell me?" she finally asked.

"Now," Livvy replied with a smile. "That's why you're all here tonight. Kevin asked this past weekend, and I said yes."

"We also found the perfect place, and we'll be moving in at the end of the month," Kevin added.

They were still congratulating the happy couple when the head server appeared with their beverages. They ordered their meals, and then went back to congratulating Kevin and Livvy.

After dinner, the questers sat around the table, enjoying the afterglow of an incredible meal.

"She never cooked this well when she was a sous chef," Nikki said. "You've inspired her to do great things, Kevin."

Kevin looked content. "She always had the skills; she just needed to be cooking for herself, not someone else."

The questers sat at the table, talking and laughing for another thirty minutes. Allison and Peter were the first to leave, since Allison had the early shift the next morning.

Nikki and Justin left next. Kevin was staying at the restaurant until closing so he could drive home with Livvy.

"Congratulations again, Kevin," Nikki said, giving him a kiss on the cheek.

"Thanks, Nikki. I think Livvy has a question to ask you, but I'll let her handle that."

Nikki tried to get him to tell her the question Livvy wanted to ask, but all Kevin would do was smile. She finally gave up, and she and Justin left the restaurant.

"Did you know Kevin proposed to Livvy?" she asked once they were inside the car.

"Only when he asked me to be his best man," Justin replied. "I had to promise not to say anything and spoil the surprise."

"And you couldn't tell me?" Nikki was surprised.

"I keep my promises," Justin replied. "Besides, Livvy should've been the one to tell you, not me."

It turned out that the question Livvy wanted to ask Nikki,

which she asked the next morning before work, was to be her maid of honor. Nikki accepted on the spot. "What kind of wedding are you thinking of, and what kind of bachelorette party do you want?"

"Small wedding," Livvy said. "And no bachelorette party, unless you, me, and Allison want to get together to watch trashy movies and eat snacks. I want to keep everything low-key."

"When is the wedding?" Nikki inquired.

"Next spring. We haven't nailed down the date yet. And as for the location, it depends on the number of guests and the weather."

"You're not thinking of an outdoor wedding are you?" Nikki was shocked at the idea.

Livvy shrugged. "We haven't decided. Outdoor weddings are high risk, so we'll have to choose the venue carefully."

Nikki and Justin signed the paperwork for their new apartment later that week. That weekend, they started moving.

Since Nikki's old apartment was just around the corner, they moved her first. Then they moved Justin. Kevin and Peter helped, as did Nikki. It took several trips to get Justin's things to the new place, and he hired movers to handle his furniture.

The last items to be put where they belonged were the game controllers that allowed Nikki, Justin, and the other questers to accept quests in the world of Annwyn. Nikki had one, and Justin had one.

"What do we do with these?" Nikki asked as they stared at the two game controllers sitting on the coffee table.

Justin shrugged. "Even if we were still accepting quests, we'd only need one."

Nikki continued staring at the controllers. "Part of me wants to get rid of them, and part of me wants to keep one of them in case we ever want to communicate with, or visit, Bethany and Thor."

Justin put his arm around Nikki's shoulder. "We don't have to decide now. Why don't I pack mine up and put it in the storage bedroom, and you hook yours up? If you want to get rid of it later, or put it in the storage bedroom with mine, you can."

Nikki nodded. She hooked her controller to the television, and Justin put his in the storage bedroom closet on the upper shelf.

When Justin returned to the living room, Nikki was opening a bottle of champagne. On the coffee table, next to the flutes, were several washcloths.

"What's all this?" he asked.

"Well, now that everything has been moved in, arranged, and put away, I thought we might want to celebrate our first night of officially living together. You, know, christen the place... break it in, so to speak."

Justin looked into Nikki's eyes and knew exactly what she meant. Her eyes, her smile, her entire body language told him everything she wanted from him at that moment, and from his body's response, he knew he wanted it, too.

"I think that's a wonderful idea," he said softly, moving toward her and slipping an arm around her waist.

Nikki handed him a champagne flute and filled it with

the bubbly liquid. She then filled her own glass, put the bottle down, and clinked the rim of her flute against his.

Justin knew that champagne had quite an effect on Nikki, and he didn't mind that at all.

Nikki felt the familiar warmth, radiating from her core and spreading out to all of her extremities. The fingers holding her champagne flute tingled, her nipples hardened, and she was getting wet between her legs. The champagne made the warmth and its effects spread faster, but it was Justin's presence that had the most profound effect on her.

They drained their glasses and placed them on the coffee table. Justin walked over to the light switches and turned them all off. When he turned back to face Nikki, she was already naked, standing in the glow from the city lights coming through the half-open blinds of the room's windows. She looked angelic in the light, but her body screamed of something else entirely.

Nikki's tall, athletic build made her the most attractive woman Justin had ever met. The skin of her body was tanned, smooth, and hairless. The gentle curve of her hips, and the shape of her breasts and her butt, were like magnets to Justin's hands. He wanted to rub her hips and clutch her butt, and he wanted to caress her breasts and her flat, toned stomach. Even her legs were so perfectly shaped that he just wanted to massage every inch of her so his hands could touch... everything.

She brushed her hand through her hair, tucking it behind her ear. Looking up at him innocently, she softly asked, "What are you waiting for?"

"I'm just enjoying the view, Nichole," he said, as he started undressing. "It's a sight I never tire of. I could just stare at your perfect body for the rest of my life and count myself as the luckiest man alive."

Nikki blushed, and her dimples showed themselves as she smiled demurely. She was still standing so he could see her profile, but she turned toward him as he finished removing his clothes. She held out her hand. He walked forward and took it.

"Where shall we begin?" she whispered.

Justin motioned toward the window.

Nikki nodded and led him there. Then she turned her back to the window and reached up. She put her arms around his broad shoulders and pulled him close. Then she rose up on her tiptoes and kissed him.

"Oh, my Nichole." Justin's arms encircled her back as they kissed, but soon his hands began exploring. They moved down and caressed her muscular butt. Then he clutched her butt cheeks and lifted her off the floor. She wrapped her legs around his waist, and, with her back against the window, held on to him as his hands moved to her breasts.

She felt his erection growing between her legs, and she reached down with one hand to stroke him so he'd be fully engorged faster. It didn't take long. She released him and reached for her clit, stimulating herself while making sure she was wet enough for his penetration.

She was, and she guided him inside of her.

Justin's hands cradled her butt, and his arms lifted her up and down, allowing him to thrust deeply while standing. Nikki began moaning immediately, enjoying the sensation of him inside of her. She continually felt amazed at the feeling of being physically connected in this way to a man, but it was their emotional connection that made the physical so much more intense, more pleasurable, more satisfying.

Nikki felt her first orgasm approaching, and she clutched Justin around his shoulders and held on tightly. The orgasm hit, and her body shook as he continued lifting her and lowering her on his erection.

When she stopped shaking, Justin released her and allowed her to stand. Then he turned her around, facing the window. She placed her hands on the metal window frame and leaned forward.

Justin penetrated her from behind. With his hands on her hips, he began thrusting. Nikki let out a loud moan as he thrust deeply.

Justin increased speed, and Nikki's moans intensified. She cried out as the second orgasm hit. Her knees shook and her ankles rolled, but Justin's hands kept her from falling and breaking the connection. He continued thrusting as she experienced orgasm after orgasm.

She watched his reflection in the window as they continued sharing pleasure. Then Justin released her hips and reached around to clutch her breasts, which were firm. Her nipples were hard as his hands stroked them. He leaned forward so his stomach pressed against her back, and he kissed her shoulders as he continued thrusting.

The next orgasm was so intense that Nikki had to clutch the windowsill to remain upright. Her upper body shook so hard that Justin had to wrap his arms around her to hang on to her.

When the shaking subsided, Nikki pushed Justin back toward the couch. She made him sit, and then she knelt in front of him. She grabbed his erection and began stroking it with her tongue, before placing it into her mouth.

She used her lips and her tongue to stimulate him as

he leaned back on the sofa and moaned softly.

But Nikki was just teasing him. She didn't want him to finish anytime soon.

Just as Justin's moans became deeper and louder, she stood, turned around, and sat on his lap, using her strong legs to lift and lower herself on his erection. Her wetness, combined with the thrusting, created a white froth that lubricated them both.

After several minutes, Nikki stood, faced Justin, and sat on him again, forcing him to penetrate her immediately. She put her arms around his neck and began moving up and down on him.

She orgasmed several times in that position, but she never stopped, except when she began shaking so hard from one orgasm that it would have put her flat on the floor had Justin not caught her and held her close to him.

Nikki rolled off of him and got on her knees on the sofa cushion next to him. He moved behind her, penetrated her, and began thrusting again. Nikki's knees trembled as her stomach muscles spasmed immediately from the most intense orgasm yet. She could barely catch her breath.

Justin felt his own release approaching. He gripped her waist and increased the speed of his thrusts.

Nikki felt his size increase just before she felt the hot liquid shooting deep inside of her. Justin cried out as he released, unwilling to pull out but unable to continue thrusting from the intensity of his own orgasm.

When he knew he was done, he reached for two of the washcloths. He pulled out, and placed one between Nikki's legs, using the other one to wipe off her froth and his cum from himself.

Nikki turned around, curled up next to him, and put

her head on his shoulder. "That... was amazing."

Justin, panting, nodded. "But we forgot to wash first."

"Plenty of time for that before round two," Nikki purred.

"Round two?"

"We still have several rooms to go. There's the bathroom, the kitchen, two bedrooms..."

"All in one night?" Justin asked.

Nikki looked up at him. "You have other plans?"

Justin smiled. "No, just making sure I know what you're expecting from me."

"More of that," she whispered. "Lots more of that."

After a short rest, and Nikki's hands working their magic on Justin, round two began. It started in the kitchen on one of the counters, moved to the master bathroom, where Justin made Nikki squirt in the shower—twice—and ended up in the bedroom, where Nikki squirted three more times, squealing loudly each time she ejaculated.

"Thank God you brought the extra towels in here," she panted after the third time. "The bed would be soaked if you hadn't."

"What did you teach me?" Justin whispered.

"Proper prior planning prevents piss-poor performance," she responded.

"Right. Now roll over."

She obliged, lying face down on the bed. Justin moved on top and penetrated her. She didn't squirt, but her orgasm came quickly and intensely.

When she stopped shaking, Justin rolled onto his back, and she climbed on top. She began moving her hips back and forth while kissing him. She increased speed until she felt him swell inside of her. A moment later, she felt him release again.

When he was finished, they grabbed the wet towels and headed back to the shower to clean off the sweat and cum before they went to sleep. But Nikki wasn't quite finished with him. She got on her knees, using her mouth and tongue on him. She looked up at him, keeping eye contact as she moved her head back and forth. When she felt she needed to stop and let her hands finish him off, she felt the familiar swelling, followed by the taste of the salty, sticky liquid shooting down her throat.

Justin cried out as he came, and when he was done, Nikki stood, facing him.

"Satisfied?"

Justin nodded, unable to speak.

"Good. Welcome home," she purred as she reached for the soap.

# CHAPTER 2

Life over the next month settled into a happy routine for Nikki and Justin—and for the rest of the questers. The three couples enjoyed living normal lives, after the adventures of their two quests. Nikki's nightmares had all but disappeared, and she no longer flinched when she heard anything that sounded like a whip cracking.

Livvy and Kevin had moved into their new home closer to the rock-wall climbing center, leaving Nikki as the only original member of the girl questers who still lived in her building. And though she missed seeing her friends almost every day, she had Justin, and he was the love of her life.

One Friday night, after a particularly long and grueling week, Nikki and Justin decided to go to bed early. Justin was wearing shorts and a t-shirt, and Nikki was wearing panties and one of Justin's t-shirts.

Well after midnight, Nikki was snuggled next to Justin

when she thought she heard the rumble of thunder. As she drifted back to sleep, she heard it again. Then she saw a blinding flash of white light coming from the living room.

Nikki and Justin sat straight up in bed. "Did you turn the game controller on?" Justin whispered.

"No. It's hasn't been on since Bethany returned to Annwyn," she responded.

There was no sound in the apartment, but then Nikki saw light coming from the television in the living room.

"Someone's in there," she whispered.

"Nikki? Nikki are you here?" It was a female voice.

Nikki started to get out of bed, but Justin caught her arm. "What are you doing?" he hissed.

Nikki pulled her arm free and grabbed the pistol she kept in her night table drawer. "I'm going to see who it is."

Nikki always kept a round in the chamber. She stood, flipped off the safety, and crept toward the living room, holding the pistol as the army taught her and as she taught her students. Justin got out of bed and followed her.

Nikki stopped and leaned against the wall next to the bedroom door, listening. There was definitely someone moving around in the living room.

"Are they there?" It was a man's voice, and it sounded familiar, for some reason.

"I don't know," the woman's voice answered. "I'll check."

Nikki held up two fingers to signal Justin that there were two people in the living room. She took a deep breath and then burst out of the bedroom. Her pistol pointed at the woman approaching her from the coffee table.

"Freeze, or I'll shoot!"

Nikki's pistol was aimed at the redhead facing her. She

recognized the woman's face instantly, but her mind wouldn't let her believe that Bethany was standing in front of her. Her ginger friend was supposed to be on another world with Thor! Then she recognized the face on the television screen. It was Ravana, the tavern owner in Riverstone.

Nikki's mind was slow to grasp what she was seeing, but she asked, "Bethany? Ravana?"

Bethany stood frozen in place, looking too terrified to make a move.

"Don't shoot!" Ravana implored. "We can explain."

"Start talking," Justin said, exiting the bedroom and moving next to Nikki.

"Can I put my hands down first?" Bethany asked.

Nikki came to her senses, flipped the safety back on the pistol, and ran forward to give her friend a hug.

"I've missed you," Nikki said. "What are you doing here?"

"I've missed you, too," Bethany answered. "And believe me, I wouldn't be here if there had been a choice."

"What are you talking about?" Justin demanded as he came over to give Bethany a hug. "Has something happened?"

"*Everything* has happened," the tavern owner replied.

Nikki looked at Bethany. "I think you need to explain."

Bethany nodded. "Yes, we need to talk. But I need to talk to all six of you. Can you get the others over here? Now?"

Nikki looked at the clock on the wall. "Bethany, it's almost three o'clock in the morning."

"I know." Bethany looked guilty and worried at the same time. "It's that important."

"Is Thor okay?" Justin asked.

Bethany nodded. "For now. But things are happening that might change that. Annwyn is on the verge of a world war. It might all go up in flames if we don't do something. That's why I'm here in person. We need your help."

Thirty minutes later, Nikki and Justin were dressed, and Livvy, Kevin, Allison, and Peter were sitting in Nikki and Justin's living room. The questers were happy to see Bethany, but there was a strong sense of foreboding when they also saw the tavern owner on the television screen.

"Someone had better have a good explanation for this," Livvy grumbled. She had on a t-shirt and jeans, but she appeared like she had just rolled out of bed. Her hair looked like the nest of a drunken bird, and in addition to looking tired, she was clearly pissed from lack of sleep.

"I'll bring all of you to Riverstone, and we can talk here," the tavern owner said.

"Oh, no you won't," Justin said. "We talk here or not at all. We're not setting foot anywhere on Annwyn until we know exactly what we're getting ourselves into and have agreed to take on whatever quest you have for us."

Bethany and the tavern owner looked at each other, and the tavern owner nodded. Bethany, still looking at the television screen, asked, "Do you want to start, or do you want me to?"

"You start," the tavern owner replied. "I'll chime in when needed."

Bethany nodded and faced the others. "Okay. First of all, you remember hearing about King Constantine, the

High King of the Eight Realms?"

The others nodded.

"Well, he was assassinated about a month ago. No one saw the assassin. By right of succession, his eldest niece, Princess Angélique, is supposed to become the High Queen of the Eight Realms. She and her armies have been deployed in the realms, putting down an unusual number of insurrections as part of their peacekeeping duties. Anyway, preparations were being made for King Constantine's funeral and Princess Angélique's coronation, when Princess Telise, her half-sister, accused Princess Angélique of murdering King Constantine."

"Did Princess Angélique murder her uncle?" Livvy asked.

Bethany shook her head. "No one thinks so. She and her armies have been moving from realm to realm, trying to restore order. It's a mess in the realms right now, but I'll come back to that later. For now, there's little chance of Princess Angélique, or one of her men, being the assassin. Most of the kings in the other realms think that Princess Telise was the assassin. Thor certainly thinks so, but mostly because of the way Telise has been behind all the attempts to seize the Portal of Alesia."

"We think she has her sights set on the Portal of Riverstone, too," the tavern owner added. "There are a large number of strangers in Riverstone all of a sudden... watching. The tavern is under constant surveillance."

"Who are these men?" Justin asked. "The same thugs who kidnapped Thor's predecessor?"

The tavern owner shook his head. "No, I believe they're from Cockaigne—Viscount Ladrach's former soldiers, probably. Rumor has it that he was working with

Princess Telise to destabilize Cockaigne, since its portal lies closest to Riverstone. Control of that portal would be vital for any attempt to conquer Riverstone and make it part of the High Kingdom's realms."

"Is that what Telise is up to?" Nikki asked.

The tavern owner nodded. "It seems so. She's hell-bent on power, to the point that I think she's willing to use her half-sister's armies to conquer all of the realms and the territories—like Riverstone and Alesia—and bring it all under her personal rule."

"So that's why she accused her half-sister of murder?" Allison asked. "So she can get control of the armies?"

Bethany nodded. "That's what Thor thinks. She's the acting High Queen, until after Angélique's trial, and since there's no proof against Angélique, other than what Telise has concocted, it's doubtful that Angélique will live to stand trial. Her death will cement Telise's claim to the High Kingdom. Thor's worried that the portals will end up being used to control the realms, rather than for transportation between the realms. He wants to shut down the portal located in the High Kingdom, but the High Kingdom's soldiers are already deployed in the other realms, so it's too late to shut down the portal to stop Telise's plans."

"And what about Princess Angélique?" Livvy asked. "What's her position in all this?"

Bethany looked uncomfortable. "Half of her armies remain loyal to her and don't believe that she murdered the High King. The other half is loyal to the High Kingdom and is following Telise's orders to capture, arrest, and return Angélique to the High Kingdom for trial and... execution."

"Angélique has gone into hiding," the tavern owner said. "And she has asked for help clearing her name. Her loyal soldiers are encamped in one of the realms, while the other army is moving from realm to realm, looking for her. They won't find her, of course, but that doesn't mean that spies might not find her and report her whereabouts."

Nikki nodded. "Because she's in Riverstone, and Viscount Ladrach's soldiers are all over the place?"

The tavern owner smiled. "Brilliant as always, Nikki-the-Warrior. You are correct. She is in Riverstone, under my protection, but I don't know how long she'll be safe here. That's why we're asking for your help."

"And now we come to it," Justin muttered. "What are you asking of us?"

"The realms are arming for war," Bethany said. "Some want to withdraw from the High Kingdom, some want to overthrow the High Kingdom, some are worried that their neighbors might invade... and with the High Kingdom's armies distracted by Telise's accusations against Angélique, there is no peacekeeping force at the moment maintaining control. The realms could go up in flames, and that would cause the most hurt to the people, not just the armies and nobles. Thor wants to intervene, but anything he does just gives Telise more justification for taking control of the portals. It's a mess over here."

"And how do we fit into all of this?" Justin demanded.

"The realms need to be united against Princess Telise's ambitions," the tavern owner replied. "She would be a terrible High Queen. At the moment, only Angélique can bring the realms together, but she's a fugitive. She needs protecting while she meets with the kings to work out a united strategy for dealing with things before Annwyn is destroyed."

"What about her soldiers?" Kevin asked. "Why can't

they protect her?"

"Because the two armies of the High Kingdom are going to end up fighting each other at some point. The army following Telise's orders is searching for the army loyal to Angélique, and they will eventually be in the same place at the same time. If Angélique is with her army, then she's either going to be preparing for a war she cannot win, or she and her army will be popping through the portals trying to remain hidden from the other army. She won't be able to plan anything with the kings if she's doing all of that. She has twenty soldiers serving as her bodyguard, but she needs more help. You are friends with the King of Cockaigne, and that's where you'll need to start. Then, with his help, you can visit the other kings, helping Angélique plan for how to end all this peacefully."

The questers looked at each other. Then Peter said, "That's a big ask, Ravana. You're asking us to risk almost certain death for a world we've only visited twice. We have our own lives to live here, you know. I understand the position that you, Thor, and Bethany are in, and I don't want to see anything happen to Cockaigne, after all we did to prevent its civil war, but you're talking about preventing a world war! That's not an easy task, regardless of whatever new powers the portal is granting us."

The other questers nodded.

Bethany looked concerned. Then she said, "You remember Ravana talking about why he recruits questers from Earth? That the simple life on Annwyn has caused the people to lose much of their creative thinking? Well, I've seen example after example of that over the past few months. Even the simplest of tasks require smarts that just aren't available. Look at all the stupid decisions and plans that Atreus made while trying to become the next Grand Master. Look at how Princess Telise's plans keep falling apart. Look at how Lord Rigderg and Duke Berngal's solution to every problem was arming for war. The list of examples is long, and it's like that all over the Eight Realms.

"The thing that makes Annwyn such a charming place is also what's tearing it apart. You six," Bethany gestured toward her friends, "have enough smarts between you to end this war before it begins and thwart Telise's plans once and for all. We need you. Thor and I need you. Angélique needs you. Please, help us. If you do... then we promise we'll never ask for your help again."

"Bethany..." the tavern owner cautioned.

"No, Ravana," Bethany said to the television screen. "They're right. This is the most we've ever asked of someone, and if they agree to help us, then it has to be the last thing we ever ask them to do. They can still reach out to us, but we can never reach out to them again. Not for quests, anyway."

"But they're the best questers we've ever had," the tavern owner protested.

"And they have their own lives to live here," Bethany reminded him. "It's all we have to bargain with."

She turned back to her friends. "Well? Will you help?"

Justin and Nikki looked at each other, and then they looked at their friends. "I say that either we all go, or we all stay," Justin said. "So if your answer is no, say so now."

No one said anything.

"Are you still thinking, or is your answer yes?" Nikki asked after a minute.

"I'm still thinking," Peter said.

"I'm still thinking," Kevin echoed.

Peter looked at Allison, and something unspoken passed between them. Then Peter said, "I've decided."

Kevin looked at Livvy, and she shrugged. He looked at Justin, and Justin could tell that Kevin was still conflicted.

Justin looked at Nikki. "What are you thinking?"

Nikki's shoulders slumped. "I don't want to go. I just don't know if I can face the possibility of what happened to me last time happening again. But I won't be the only no vote. If everyone else votes yes, then I'll go, even though I'm not thrilled about this."

Justin nodded. He looked at the others. "Has everyone made up their minds?"

Everyone but Nikki and Kevin nodded.

"Okay." Justin held out his left fist, thumb pointing sideways. The others did the same. "I'll count to three. When I say 'three,' give a thumbs up if you want to go, and a thumbs down if you want to stay."

The others nodded.

"One. Two. Three."

Justin, Allison, Peter, and Livvy gave a thumbs up. Kevin looked at Livvy for a moment, and then he slowly gave a thumbs up, too.

Nikki looked at the others and then looked at Justin. There was pain in her eyes. "Vote the way you feel, not the way anyone else voted," Justin whispered. "Only you know if you can do this."

"You're not going without me," Nikki said. "Just like I'd never go without you."

Justin reached for Nikki's hand and put his hands around hers. "Then we ether go together or we stay together. Your choice. I support whatever you decide."

Nikki felt her heart beating faster at the thought of returning to Annwyn. It was the last place she wanted to be, despite her nightmares lessening with each passing week. The memories were still there. The place where it happened was still there.

She felt Justin's calm reassurance making her feel safe. Even the warmth of his hands around hers gave her confidence that she'd never have to face anything alone again. She looked into his eyes and saw his love and devotion to her—all of the things she felt for him.

She nodded, and Justin let go of her hand. She gave a thumbs up.

"It's decided," Justin said to Bethany. "We're going. But know this. If anything as terrible as what happened last time happens to Nikki on this quest, I'll unleash the beast again, but I won't just kill the people responsible for hurting her. Is that understood?"

Bethany, wide-eyed, nodded, as did the tavern owner.

The tavern owner asked, "Is everyone ready for the journey here?"

Everyone nodded and stood. The familiar thunder rolled in the distance. Then they heard it again, sounding much closer. The room filled with blinding white light, and the living room disappeared.

# The Quest Begins

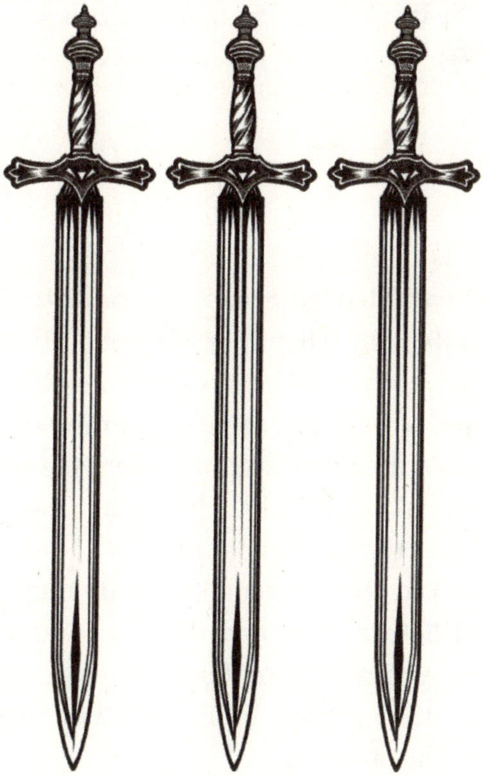

# CHAPTER 3

The tavern looked exactly the same to the questers and Bethany when they arrived in Riverstone. The tables and benches were the same, the barrels and bottles of spirits were the same, the exposed beams were the same... even the floors and walls were the same.

The tavern owner and his four assistants were standing behind the bar, watching.

Nikki looked around to make certain that all six of the questers and Bethany had arrived. Everyone was standing with her in the center of the floor, dressed as they always were when the portal brought them from Nikki's apartment to the tavern.

The air was chilly inside the tavern, in spite of the fire roaring in the oversized fireplace. Nikki was grateful for the heavy wool traveling cloak she was wearing. She was particularly grateful that it was hooded.

She checked her weapons and her armor. Everything seemed the same as the last time she stood in the tavern.

She glanced at Justin, who seemed as uneasy as she felt about being back.

"Greetings, Bethany," the tavern owner said.

"Greetings, Ravana," she replied.

"Greetings courageous questers," the tavern owner said to the Nikki and the others.

"Ravana," Justin said with a nod. "Are our horses here?"

"Indeed, yes," the tavern owner replied. "They're saddled and hitched out back. All you need is your supplies, which are in the usual place."

"Tell us about these men you think were Viscount Ladrach's former soldiers," Nikki asked.

"They started arriving right about the time you left us," the tavern owner replied. "They appeared to be merchants, wagoneers, travelers, and different kinds of tradesmen. But they all carry themselves like military men, and they all have the accent of northern Cockaigne. Since you destroyed their former employer on your first quest here, it stands to reason that they'd seek employment from someone else. There's little chance of finding employment in their own realm; they're all wanted men in Cockaigne."

"And they're watching this place?"

"Constantly," the tavern owner replied.

"Then how do we leave without being seen?" Justin asked.

"Darkness and speed are your only aides... unless you want Livvy-the-Sorceress to make you all invisible for your journey," the tavern owner replied, "although the horses won't like that at all. Personally, I'd leave here a few at a time and meet somewhere between the tavern and the farmhouse where Angélique is waiting. My assistants can retrieve your supplies from the shed, bring them in here, and you can take them outside to your horses when you leave. With luck, the watchers will either be less than vigilant, or they'll think you've been staying here at the tavern and are not new arrivals."

Livvy and Kevin looked at each other. "I think we do what Ravana suggested, but one of us takes the form of a night bird to provide aerial reconnaissance."

"You want to be an owl?" Livvy asked with a smile.

Kevin nodded. "I've done it before. I can tell you what I see, and you can relay that to the others. It covers all the bases without taxing your powers, which I think we're going to need more than ever on this quest."

Justin nodded in agreement. "It's a good plan."

The others agreed.

"All right," the tavern owner said. "We'll get your supplies and be back in a few minutes."

Ravana and his assistants headed out the back of the tavern to the supply shed.

Bethany wasn't smiling, and Nikki walked up to her. "What's wrong?"

Bethany looked at Nikki and tried to smile. "I just hate bringing you back here like this. I was hoping you could come back and visit for the wedding, but that has been put off until this other mess can be dealt with."

"You're getting married?" Allison said. "That's great. Peter and I eloped a couple of months ago, and we love being married. Livvy and Kevin are engaged, too."

Bethany looked at the others wide-eyed. "That's great!" Looking at Nikki, she started to ask about her and Justin, but Nikki interrupted her.

"Justin and I are living together now, and we're

planning for our future, but we haven't formalized anything beyond our address yet."

Bethany nodded, but she was smiling broadly now.

The tavern owner and his assistants arrived with the first load of supplies, including bedrolls, weapons, and other gear they'd need on the road as winter approached. He and two of his assistants went back to the shed to get the rest while the other assistants headed into the kitchen to gather water and rations.

Once all of the supplies and rations had been retrieved, the questers loaded their saddlebags and prepared to secure the rest to their saddles.

"One of my assistants, Thomas here, will lead you to the farmhouse and back again," the tavern owner said. Thomas was wearing a heavy leather jerkin underneath his wool-and-fur traveling cloak, but he carried no visible weapons.

Nikki looked at Justin. "I hate suggesting this, but you and I should go separately, in case there's trouble. We'll meet at the rendezvous."

Justin nodded. He, Livvy, Bethany, and Thomas would be in the first group to leave. Nikki, Allison, and Peter would be in the second group. Thomas would lead Kevin's horse, and he'd escort Bethany back to the tavern once she had met with Angélique and passed along her message from Thor.

Justin gave Nikki a kiss, and then he stepped outside to secure his supplies to his horse.

Livvy transformed Kevin into a beautiful barn owl, who hopped up on her arm. "Remember, keep in constant contact, okay?"

Kevin hooted in response, but via their mental

connection, he said, *"I will. I love you."*

*"I love you, too."*

Livvy, Bethany, and Thomas followed Justin out the rear door. Livvy carried Kevin on her arm, and once outside, she raised her arm, and the owl took off to begin looking for anyone watching or following the group.

There were close to thirty of the late Viscount Ladrach's men camped in the vicinity of the tavern that night. Five were on duty, watching the tavern, while the others were resting. Two watched the front, one watched the back, and the other two watched the sides. Only one saw Justin, Livvy, Bethany, and Thomas leave.

The watcher ran around to the front of the tavern to report to his sergeant.

"Heading south, eh?" the sergeant asked when the watcher told what he had seen. "Did you recognize any of them?"

"I sure did," the watcher responded. "There was a redhead... you don't forget a bird like that. She was one of the strangers who killed Viscount Ladrach and destroyed his castle. I'd never forget her."

The sergeant nodded. "Any of the others?"

"There was a woman with a rapier," he replied, referring to Livvy. "She was holding a bird of some sort when she came out of the tavern, but she let it fly off when she mounted her horse. She was at Viscount Ladrach's castle when it was destroyed, too... same as the redhead."

The sergeant thought about this. He had personal reasons to want to find anyone responsible for Viscount

Ladrach's death, but he also had orders from the spymaster of the High Kingdom: find any strangers who might be in Riverstone to help Princess Angélique, and be on the lookout for any redheads. Princess Telise had put a bounty on redheads, and the sergeant was determined to collect it.

"Wake the others," he said to the other man watching the front of the tavern. "I want ten men watching the tavern. The rest will go with me to see about these people who left the tavern. We want the redhead and anyone else who was there when the Viscount was defeated. If any of the others get in our way, then we'll show them how Viscount Ladrach's men get their revenge."

Kevin saw the men watching the tavern and reported this to Livvy. Then he saw the watcher at the rear of the tavern leave his post and run to the men watching the front of the tavern. He swooped down silently to hear what they were saying.

When he heard the sergeant say that they wanted to capture Bethany, and possibly Livvy, he informed Livvy immediately. Then he flew higher so he could watch what they did next.

A few minutes after Livvy, Justin, Bethany, and Thomas left the tavern, Nikki heard Livvy's voice inside her head.

*"Can you hear me, Nikki?"*

*"I can year you, Livvy."*

*"Kevin says that there are about thirty men watching*

*the tavern, but the man watching the rear left his post to report seeing us leave. There's no one watching the rear right now. If you hurry, you can be gone before anyone knows you were ever there."*

*"Right. Leaving now. Thanks, Livvy!"*

Nikki informed Peter and Allison what Livvy had said. They grabbed their supplies and headed for the rear door.

"Take a right out of here and stay on the main road heading south until you reach a fork," the tavern owner said. "Take the left fork, cross the stream, and keep right from then on. I told Thomas to wait for you at the second crossroad after the stream."

Nikki nodded. "Will do. See you soon."

She and the others loaded their gear onto their horses, mounted, and rode after the others.

"Good luck, Courageous Questers," the tavern owner said as he watched them ride away.

Kevin watched as twenty mounted thugs rode south, looking for Bethany and Livvy. Several were carrying torches. It made them visible from a distance, but it was the only way to find and follow the questers' trail in the darkness. The waning moon had not yet risen, and the sky was quite dark.

Kevin could see Justin's group and Nikki's group riding south, and he could tell that the late Viscount's men had picked up their trail and were following.

*"Livvy, they're following your tracks."*

*"Thanks, Kevin. When Nikki and her group catch up to us, I'll make our tracks disappear and leave false trails*

*that'll keep them busy for hours."*

*"Good plan."*

Kevin saw Justin's group arrive at the rendezvous point. A few minutes later, Nikki and her group arrived. Thomas then led them all to the farmhouse where Princess Angélique was hiding.

Kevin flew between the questers and the late Viscount's men so he could watch both groups. When the late Viscount's men reached the rendezvous point, they looked around and then changed direction, following one of Livvy's false trails in the opposite direction.

*"They're heading away from you,"* he reported to Livvy.

He watched the late Viscount's men take several wrong turns. Satisfied that they'd be busy and lost for some time, he flew after the questers to make certain that the way forward was clear of any dangers.

He caught up to the questers as they approached a cluster of farmhouses well away from the road they had been following. He saw movement around one of the farmhouses, and he swooped down to investigate. As he dropped lower, he saw men patrolling around one of the farmhouses. He increased altitude and began circling.

*"Livvy, there are men ahead of you."*

*"Where?"*

*"Second farmhouse on the left. They're all wearing black traveling cloaks. These look like professional men, not your average thugs."*

Livvy was silent for a minute. Then she said, *"Thomas says those are Princess Angélique's men. We've arrived."*

Kevin flew down and landed on the saddle of his horse. Livvy smiled at him and transformed him back into his human form. Thomas tossed Kevin the reins to his horse.

"Good to see you again," Livvy whispered.

"Good to be here," Kevin replied.

They rode toward the second farmhouse on the left. As they approached, several of the men that Kevin had seen moved to block their path—swords drawn and bows at the ready.

"State your name and your business," the captain of the guards ordered.

"It's Thomas," said Thomas to the man. "From the tavern at Riverstone."

"No one move until we can verify that."

A torch was called for, and it arrived a minute later.

When the captain of the guards recognized Thomas, he said, "You work for the Portal Keeper in Riverstone, yes?"

Thomas nodded. "Yes. I brought the people Ravana spoke about."

The captain lifted his torch and looked at the others. "They'll have to dismount and disarm before they can enter the house."

"As long as our weapons are nearby," Nikki said coldly. "There are men out there who used to work for Viscount Ladrach of Cockaigne, and they're trying to capture several of us. I don't plan to be caught defenseless."

The captain regarded Nikki for a moment. Then he said, "Okay, your weapons can go inside the house, but you cannot have them on you when you meet with... our leader."

"Fine," Nikki said, dismounting. "And the horses need to be kept out of sight in case the Viscount's men should ride by. No sense advertising that we're here. That would be bad for both us... and your leader." As the horses were led away, she added, "Leave the bows and quivers alone." They were still attached to the saddles of four of the horses.

The captain nodded and gave orders to his men. Then he led the questers, Bethany, and Thomas to the house. When they reached the porch, he said, "You *do* know who you're about to meet, don't you?"

"Yes, we do," Nikki replied. "And you know that we're not subjects of the High Kingdom or any of the Eight Realms?"

The captain nodded.

"Good," Nikki said. "Let's not keep her waiting any longer than necessary."

"Nicely handled," Justin whispered in Nikki's ear.

"Ten years as a soldier teaches you a few things," she whispered back.

They entered the house, along with eight of the soldiers and the captain of the guard. The rest of the soldiers returned to their patrol outside the farmhouse.

The captain of the guard looked sternly at Nikki and held out his hand. Nikki nodded and handed over her sword and her dagger. The others also disarmed. The weapons were leaned against the wall next to the front door.

Once the questers had been searched for any additional weapons, the captain of the guard led them to a room in the back of the house.

"Wait here," he said when they reached the doorway.

They stopped, waiting.

The captain entered the room and cleared his throat. The sole occupant of the room, a woman wearing the uniform of a General of the Army of the High Kingdom, glanced up from the map she was studying. Even at a distance, Nikki and the others could see that she was beautiful, with long auburn hair—braided to keep it away from her face—hazel eyes, and a lean yet elegant face. Her voice, clearly accustomed to command, sounded tired.

"What is it, Captain?" she asked.

"General, the people that the Portal Keeper of Riverstone sent have arrived."

She nodded and stood. "Show them in."

The captain signaled for the others to follow him into the room. The soldiers also entered and took positions around the room to protect the Princess.

Nikki, having been duped by shapeshifters before, concentrated on the woman, but her form remained the same. *At least this one seems to be the real Princess Angélique.*

"Your names?" the Princess demanded.

Thomas made the introductions. "General, may I present Nikki-the-Warrior and Justin-the-Warrior-Berserker, the leaders of the group." Nikki and Justin nodded to the Princess. Thomas continued. "This is Livvy-the-Sorceress, Allison-the-Healer, Peter-the-Warrior, and Kevin-the-Rogue-Assassin."

Thomas then presented Bethany. "This is Bethany-the-Healer, who is also the Grand Master's betrothed. She was once a member of this group, but she now lives in Alesia. She has a message from the Grand Master that she is here to deliver."

Thomas then gestured to Angélique. "Allow me to introduce you to Princess Angélique, rightful High Queen of the Eight Realms and General of the armies of the High Kingdom."

The questers nodded to her.

Princess Angélique flashed a tired smile. "All those titles could parch the throat. I prefer to be called 'General,' if you don't mind. Thank you all for coming. I assume you've been briefed on what we're facing?"

"The basic facts, yes," Thomas answered.

"Good." Angélique looked at Bethany. "Can you deliver your message in front of everyone else, or is it for my ears only?"

"I can deliver it in front of everyone, General."

"Proceed," Angélique requested.

"The Grand Master is deeply concerned, General," Bethany began. "War between the realms and the High Kingdom is not in anyone's best interest, but that is what we're currently facing. The corruption of your late uncle and your half-sister has been tearing apart the peace that has been the hallmark of Annwyn for centuries. Your forces, which were formerly a peacekeeping force, have turned into the iron hand of the tyranny of the High Kingdom, enforcing the will of your uncle, and now your half-sister, against the realms. Your half-sister's repeated attempts to seize control of the portals are intolerable, and now her declaring you as the culprit for a murder that she has committed is the last straw.

"The Portal Keepers have historically kept out of the politics within the realms, but they cannot remain neutral any longer. To prevent a war that would engulf our world, the Portal Keepers are prepared to shut down all of the portals in the Eight Realms, isolating the realms and the High Kingdom until such time as your half-sister is banished from Annwyn and new treaties between the realms can be drafted and ratified that will help ensure nothing like this ever happens again."

Angélique leapt to her feet. "They'll what?"

Bethany held up her hand. "There's more, if you'll allow me to finish."

Angélique glared at Bethany. Then Angélique sat down and gestured for Bethany to continue.

"Since the Grand Master believes that your half-sister is the worst calamity Annwyn has ever experienced, he and the Portal Keepers are willing to help you reclaim your crown and depose Princess Telise. He wishes to meet with you, in Alesia, to make plans that will be in the best interest of the people and the realms. He suggests you convince the kings of the other realms to attend as well. Frankly, Alesia is the only safe place to hold such a conference, thanks to your sister's spies roaming around all over the realms and Riverstone. If the realms can be united under a single plan, a single strategy, it could prevent a war that will only end with the blood of innocent millions spilled for no good reason."

Angélique stared at Bethany for a minute. "The Grand Master wants to help me?"

Bethany nodded. "He sees you as the best hope for a lasting peace, but it's going to require some changes, and that's not going to be easy. Convincing the kings to attend, who have known nothing but tyranny from your family for so long, will be difficult. You'll have to be willing to make—and honor—a number of concessions to gain their trust and respect. The Eight Realms won't look the same as they do

now when this crisis is over, nor will they interact the same way, but peace requires unity, and unity will require changes. If you're willing to make those changes, all of our goals can be met. Otherwise, the Grand Master will have no choice but to close the portals and isolate the realms. That will mean the end of the High Kingdom's existence and its rule over the other realms. You have to understand, General, that the Grand Master is more concerned about saving innocent lives than preserving political structures. And he has the power to enforce his will, even though he would prefer not to. The choice is yours: create a new peace with the realms, or watch the High Kingdom crumble and vanish from the memory of the realms forever."

Angélique leaned back in her chair. The captain of the guard and his soldiers shifted nervously in the silence. They weren't accustomed to receiving threats—particularly threats that they couldn't combat.

Finally, Angélique spoke. "He isn't leaving me much choice, is he?"

Bethany flashed a grim smile. "I'm afraid not, General. Unlike his predecessors, the new Grand Master is both a student of history and a very powerful sorcerer. He knows what will happen if you don't bring positive change between the realms and the High Kingdom, and he is prepared to prevent that at all costs. Believe me when I tell you that he will do as he says, but he is also willing to help you, provided you eliminate the corruption and tyranny that has become synonymous with the High Kingdom. He can be your greatest ally, but he can also be the end of your realm and your family's reign over the other realms."

Angélique nodded. "And how does he propose that I convince the other realms to meet with me and solve our problems together? If the realms hate the High Kingdom so much, why would they trust me? They'd be more likely to hang me."

Bethany gestured toward her companions. "The Grand Master suggests starting in Cockaigne. My companions are the ones who prevented its recent civil war, and the new king, Rigderg, owes his crown to them. He'll listen to them, and in turn, he may listen to you. If he likes what he hears, and he trusts you, then he may convince others to listen to you. Look at it this way, it can't hurt to try. And if it doesn't work, the Grand Master has another way to get them to come together and meet with you."

"How," Angélique demanded.

"General, you don't want to know," Bethany said.

# CHAPTER 4

Princess Telise had almost a hundred of the late Viscount Ladrach's soldiers working as spies across Riverstone, looking for the people who interfered with her plans in Cockaigne and Alesia, as well as anyone who might be helping her half-sister, Princess Angélique.

The Princess, now the acting High Queen of the Eight Realms, listened to her finance minister drone on about the state of the High Kingdom's treasury. Evidently, her late uncle had managed to drain more of the treasury than Telise realized, leaving almost nothing, apart from what was needed to support the armies. All of her planned spending—extravagances, lavish parties and ceremonies, and new clothes—would have to be put on hold indefinitely. This did not please her at all.

"Why can't we shift money from the armies to other projects," she demanded, interrupting the aging minister.

"Because, your Highness, if we stop paying the

soldiers, they'll stop fighting for us and potentially turn their swords toward us," the finance minister replied. "Men fight for money, and if we start withholding it from them, they'll storm the palace and take it from us."

"And what about our gold mines? That was the primary source of our wealth for centuries."

The finance minister shook his head. "Your uncle cut back on the mining operations to increase the size of the armies and the city garrison. It'll take months to get the mines running at full capacity again, assuming we can retrieve the trained miners from their current duties."

"Then what about taxes and tribute from the realms?"

"Your Highness, that's why the armies are deployed in the realms at the moment. The realms have stopped paying taxes and tribute to us. Until that is reestablished, we have no revenue coming in at all. And don't forget, half of your army is loyal to your sister, and the other half is loyal to the High Kingdom. One half of the army is busy looking for the other half and your sister—on your orders—which is keeping them from forcing the realms to start paying the taxes and tribute they owe."

Telise threw her hands in the air. "Why are we paying the soldiers who are loyal to my sister? We should stop paying them, as long as they're not being loyal to the needs of the High Kingdom."

"Your Highness, we've already stopped paying them—on your orders—especially since we have no idea where they are. The numbers I shared with you take into account that only half of the army is currently receiving pay."

Telise turned angrily toward the army liaison with the royal council. "Colonel, why do we need the entire loyal half of the army out looking for my sister and the disloyal half? Why can't we split the loyal half into two... divisions: one looking for my sister and the disloyal half of the army, and the other forcing the realms to pay their tribute and taxes again?"

The Colonel cleared his throat. "Your Highness, breaking the loyal half of the army won't leave enough men to convince the realms to do anything. Nothing less than the entire army has ever been enough to compel the realms to obey royal decrees. And if we break the loyal army in two pieces, and send one piece to find the disloyal half of the army, it will be outnumbered two-to-one, and should a fight break out, we'll lose that piece, and your sister will control an army twice the size of yours. They could return to the High Kingdom and depose you with little effort, and we'd be powerless to stop them."

Telise looked at her spymaster. "Any word on my sister's whereabouts or the others I want found?"

"No, your Highness," the spymaster replied. He was perhaps the only member of the council that Telise actually trusted. "The spies in the realms haven't seen her or her army, and the spies watching key places across Riverstone haven't reported in yet. It's a long ride from Riverstone to Cockaigne, which is the closest and only accessible portal they can use to get messages to us, so it takes time to get reports from those spies."

Telise fumed and then waved her hand dismissively, letting her ministers know that the meeting was over. They all stood, bowed to her, and filed out of the council chamber.

Telise watched them leave with growing irritation.

*"I should have killed Uncle Constantine years ago before he let things get this bad. He spent, I spent, and we*

*both left Angélique to run the kingdom. Now he's dead, and I framed Angélique for his murder, so there's no one left to run the kingdom but me and these idiot councilors.*

*"I need to find someone to run things for me. I wanted to be High Queen for the power, not for these administrative headaches. I need the army focused on conquering the realms so I rule all of Annwyn and can force taxes to be paid to me. But the army can't do what I need it to do with Angélique still free and alive. Half of the army is out there doing... what? Disobeying me, that's what. And the other half is looking for them. What happens if they meet? Will they wipe each other out? If that happens, the High Kingdom will cease to exist. No, I need the army intact to carry out my plans, which means the spies I have out there must find Angélique and kill her. Then I'll execute the officers of the disloyal half of the army, and welcome their soldiers back if they'll swear loyalty to me."*

Telise looked around the empty council chamber. *"But first, I need someone to handle all this administrative crap for me. If I have to listen to these old men prattle on one more time, I swear I'll call for the executioner and remove their heads."*

Telise left the council chamber and headed back to her apartment, where her slave master was waiting. Slavery was technically illegal everywhere on Annwyn, but with enough gold, and the use of certain drugs, there were willing fools who would gladly sell their soul for a night with the High Queen of the Eight Realms, and her slave master was accomplished at finding them for her. *"I wonder what diversions he has for me tonight..."*

The men from the late-Viscount Ladrach's army, who had followed Justin and the others from the tavern, were still riding around the countryside of Riverstone, trying to pick up the trail left by the questers. The sergeant, who was responsible for watching the tavern, was growing more and more irritable by the minute. Every trail they followed abruptly stopped, and when they tried to retrace their path, they discovered that the tracks they had been following were completely gone. It was infuriating.

"Can you see any sign that they came this way?" the sergeant asked his men.

"There's no sign of them," one of his men—an expert tracker—replied. "The tracks just stop. They don't turn, they don't start going backwards, they just... stop. It's unnatural."

"Sorcery, more like it," another one of his men muttered.

"What's that?" the sergeant demanded.

"Well, you remember what happened to the Viscount's castle, don't you? Only sorcery could do that. If this bunch is the same one that killed the Viscount, then there's sorcery afoot around here, like there was then."

The sergeant nodded. "Well, they can't all be sorcerers, can they? We want the redhead for Princess Telise. Any of the others who were responsible for the Viscount's demise... well, we want them for sport. But we won't get neither if we can't find them!"

"Then let's go back to the last place we know they were and wait for them to come back," the tracker suggested. "If we can intercept them before they reach the tavern, no one will ever know we took them."

"And if they don't head back to the tavern?" the sergeant demanded.

The tracker shrugged.

The sergeant nodded. "I thought so. But you're right. There's nothing to lose at this point. We don't know where they are, so we might as well find a place to watch for them in case they come back."

He signaled for his men to follow him back toward the tavern.

Bethany glanced at the map that Angélique was studying and smiled. It was a map of the Eight Realms plus Riverstone, but it didn't include Alesia. *Thor will be glad to know that Angélique doesn't know where Alesia is.*

"I need to return to the Grand Master," Bethany said. "He'll be expecting me." She turned to Thomas. "Are you ready to lead me back?"

Thomas nodded.

Bethany turned to Angélique. "Is there any message you wish me to convey for you?"

Angélique nodded. "Tell the Grand Master that I will try what he suggested."

Bethany smiled and nodded.

"But before you go, I have a question," Angélique said.

"What question is that?"

Angélique pointed to the map. "If I'm going to Alesia to meet with the kings of the realms, how do I get there if I don't know where it is?"

"The Portal Keepers know how to get you there,"

Bethany replied.

"And if I can't get to a portal?" Angélique countered.

"Then you can't get there, General."

"I want to know where Alesia is," the General demanded.

Bethany pointed at the map. "Isn't it listed there?"

"No, it's not."

"Then I guess you're not supposed to know where it is, General," Bethany said.

Angélique started to protest, but Bethany held up her hand. "My understanding is that the location of Alesia has been a secret since the portals were first built. I also believe that preserving that secret, and preserving the independence of the Portal Keepers, is written into the charter creating the Eight Realms. You're not supposed to know where it is, and after your half-sister's attempts to seize the master portal, the Grand Master will never allow you or anyone else from the High Kingdom to ever know Alesia's exact location."

Angélique glared at her but said nothing. Evidently, she was not used to her demands being refused.

Bethany turned to her friends. "It was good to see you all again. I hope we can get together when this is all over."

"So do we," Nikki said, giving her friend a hug.

Bethany hugged each of the questers, and then she left the room with Thomas, accompanied by two soldiers, who had been ordered to take Bethany and Thomas to their horses.

Angélique looked at the others. "Is she always so stubborn?" she asked, referring to Bethany.

"Very much so, General," Nikki answered. "But in this case, she's acting as an emissary for the Grand Master of the Portal Keepers, and he's even more stubborn when it comes to the safety of Alesia. Your sister committed a number of crimes when she tried to gain control of the Portal of Alesia—kidnapping, murder, attempted murder, bringing troops through the portals into Alesia, coopting a Portal Keeper. By the way, the former Portal Keeper of the High Kingdom was banished to another world for his participation in her plans, as was the shapeshifting kidnapper she used. That's how seriously the Grand Master takes the security of Alesia, and since Bethany is his betrothed, she takes it equally seriously."

Angélique nodded. Then she looked at the others. "So you're the ones who prevented civil war in Cockaigne. I'd like to know how you accomplished that."

Nikki gestured for Livvy to share the story.

Bethany and Thomas rode back to the tavern so Bethany could return to Alesia. Thomas carried a torch so they could see the road more clearly.

"You handled yourself quite well back there, ma'am," Thomas said.

"Thank you, Thomas. The Princess isn't a bad person; she's just used to things working a certain way, and she doesn't like it when she finds herself unable to control what goes on around her. Maybe some good will come from all of this if she learns a little humility."

Thomas snorted. "A member of her family learning humility? That would take a miracle."

"Stranger things have happened," Bethany noted.

They rode on in silence.

The sergeant and his men heard horses approaching.

"How many horses?" the sergeant asked his tracker.

The tracker listened for a moment, and then replied, "Two for certain."

"We were following more than two horses," the sergeant said. "There should be four, if this is the people we were following."

"Maybe the others are staying somewhere else," one of the other men suggested.

The sergeant looked around. "All right. Stay hidden in the trees. If this is the redhead or one of the others involved in the Viscount's destruction, we take them. Otherwise, we let them ride on."

The sergeant and his men waited, and soon he saw the light from Thomas' torch.

"Are they the ones you saw leave the tavern?" the sergeant asked the watcher, who was at the rear of the tavern when the first group of questers left.

"Yeah, that's them, all right."

"And is that the redhead you saw at the Viscount's castle?" the sergeant asked.

The watcher nodded. "That's her. No mistake."

As Thomas and Bethany rode closer, the sergeant whistled, and his men left their hiding places and surrounded the two.

"What is the meaning of this?" Thomas demanded, using his torch to keep the men from getting too close.

The sergeant rode forward, stopping directly in front of Bethany and Thomas. "You won't remember us," he said to Bethany, "but we remember you. You were there when Viscount Ladrach's castle was destroyed and he was killed. We were his loyal soldiers. Now we work for Princess Telise, and she has a bounty on your head. You're coming with us. We're taking you to the High Kingdom. I don't know why the Princess wants you, but we're gonna collect our reward just the same. Now, you can come along peaceful like, or you can resist, but you're coming with us either way."

Thomas moved to thrust his torch at the sergeant, but one of the Viscount's men backhanded Thomas across the face. He fell from his horse and lay on the ground, unmoving.

The sergeant looked at Bethany. "How do you want to be treated, missy?"

"I'll come peacefully," she said. She pointed at Thomas. "Just don't hurt him. He was only doing what I paid him to do."

The sergeant nodded. "Fine." He signaled his men to form up around Bethany, and then he rode north for Cockaigne.

Thomas wasn't exactly unconscious when he hit the ground, but he wasn't completely aware either. He heard Bethany agree to go with the men who surrounded them, and he remembered hearing something about her being taken to the High Kingdom. Since these men would never be able to use the Portal of Riverstone, he realized they must be heading for the Portal of Cockaigne.

*"I wonder if they know that the Grand Master moved*

*Cockaigne's portal closer to King Rigderg's castle."*

His horse began to nuzzle him. Thomas reached up and caught the reins. Then he grabbed the stirrup and pulled himself up and into the saddle. He swooned from the pain in his shoulder and his forehead, and the horse set off in the darkness. Thomas didn't know what direction the horse was taking, and he was too woozy to care.

Livvy had just finished relating the tale of how the questers had defeated Viscount Ladrach and destroyed his castle, and how they had defeated Telise's attempts to have the master portal seized, when the questers heard a shout from the soldiers outside.

Angélique leaped to her feet. "Find out what's happening," she commanded one of the soldiers in the room.

"Yes, General." The soldier left quickly.

A moment later, the captain entered the room. "Thomas, the man who works for the Portal Keeper of Riverstone, is back. He has been injured, and he's in a bad way."

"Take me to him," Allison said.

The captain pointed to one of the soldiers. "Take her to the entry hall."

The soldier led Allison out of the room.

"What about Bethany?" Nikki asked.

"There's no sign of her," the captain replied.

The questers and Angélique followed the captain to the entryway of the farmhouse. Thomas was lying on the floor, and Allison was tending to a nasty cut over one eye, a split lip, and a massive bruise on one cheek.

"What did that?" Justin asked.

"It looks like he was struck in the face by a massive hand," Allison replied. "It also looks like he fell from his horse. His shoulder is bruised and possibly sprained."

"Can he talk?" Nikki asked.

Allison shook her head. "I gave him something for the pain, and he passed out. Let me finish treating his wounds, and I'll see if I can wake him."

"Not necessary," Livvy said. She knelt next to Thomas and placed her hand on his forehead. Then she concentrated.

A moment later, she looked up at Kevin. "I need you to think about the men you saw following us," she commanded. Then she stared at him and concentrated.

After a minute, she nodded. "Thanks, Kevin. Thomas and Bethany were intercepted by twenty of Viscount Ladrach's men—the ones who tried to follow us here. They said there's a bounty on Bethany's head, and they're going to take her back to the High Kingdom to collect on it."

Livvy looked at Angélique. "If your half-sister knows that Bethany is betrothed to Thor, this could be another way Telise is attempting to exert leverage over the Grand Master."

"We need to rescue her," Nikki said. "Thor will never give in to pressure from Telise, even if it involves Bethany. Taking Bethany to the High Kingdom is a death sentence." Nikki looked at Livvy. "Did you get anything else from Thomas?"

"Yes," Livvy replied. "Cockaigne is the nearest portal they can use. Thor moved the Portal of Cockaigne from King Diarmaid's ruined castle to King Rigderg's castle a month ago. If Bethany's kidnappers don't know that, then they'll be heading for the old location of the portal. That might let us get ahead of them or give us a great place for an ambush."

"We don't have a minute to lose," Justin said. "We need to head for Cockaigne immediately."

"I'm going with you," Angélique said.

"General, you can't!" the captain of the guard said.

"I have no choice," Angélique replied. "I need to see the King of Cockaigne, and these people have to make the introduction. Plus, this woman was captured while trying to help me. I can't let that go unavenged. And these people will be outnumbered. I have to go."

"Then we're going with you," the captain stated. "We've sworn to protect you at all costs. We can't let you go out exposed and defenseless."

Angélique looked at Nikki, who nodded. "The extra soldiers can't hurt," Nikki said, "but we should separate them into three groups: one riding ahead of us, looking for anyone trying to intercept us, one riding with us to protect you, General, and one riding behind us to take care of any potential pursuit."

"And I'll change your appearance so you won't be recognized, General," Livvy added. "That will be an added protection that no one will be able to see through."

Angélique agreed, and she ordered her soldiers to gather supplies and prepare the horses.

In less than an hour, the questers, Thomas, Angélique, and her soldiers were riding north toward the tavern. They needed to help Thomas return to the protection of the tavern owner, and then they needed to go after Bethany.

Livvy transformed Angélique into the likeness of

someone she used to work with at her previous restaurant. Then she and Kevin transformed into owls to search for Bethany and any traps that might be waiting for them ahead.

Angélique rode next to Nikki, with Justin and the captain of the guard riding just ahead of them.

"What was it like when Livvy transformed you into me?" Angélique asked, finally asking the question that had her curious ever since Livvy relayed that detail.

Nikki grinned. "It was fun. I was a soldier for ten years, and I've noticed that, when soldiers get confused, they need someone strong and forceful to start issuing orders. So that's what I did. I started ordering the soldiers around, keeping them distracted until we could spring our trap on Atreus, who was also impersonating you."

"I remember him, slightly," Angélique commented. "He was one of Telise's playthings, but I had no idea he was a shapeshifter or that he was drafting my soldiers to do his bidding."

"He did a lot more than that," Nikki said, wincing at the memory of being tortured by Atreus' men.

"Yes, Livvy mentioned that you were nearly killed," Angélique said. "Barbaric. I'm surprised you're here."

"I wouldn't be, if it weren't for Bethany and Thor, the Grand Master. They're friends, and I'll do anything for my friends."

Angélique thought about this for a moment. "I've never met anyone who'd sacrifice so much for friendship. I've known patriots who'd sacrifice for king and realm, I've known soldiers who'd sacrifice for pay, but friendship? I guess I've never really had friends, so I don't know what someone would do for a friend."

"It must be a lonely life, being surrounded by people all the time and yet not being close to any of them."

"You've lived the soldier's life, Nikki, so you know how lonely it can be. But it's necessary, and it's my calling, so I do it. I just never really stopped to think about it before."

"When my unit was wiped out, and I was waiting to die, I had a lot of time to think about it," Nikki said. "That's when I decided that I was done being a soldier. I didn't want to die having never savored what life had to offer, so when I was finally rescued and healed, I left the army and tried to start living for a change. And when I met Justin, he showed me just how wonderful life could be. I owe everything to him."

"I wish I could experience that," Angélique said. "But I have too many responsibilities to walk away from duty."

"I get that," Nikki noted. "You were born into a life. I wasn't. I have the right to choose. You don't. But life, happiness, joy, they can all be found, no matter what you're born into. You can find it, you'll just have to... realign certain priorities to make space for it."

Angélique was silent for a moment. Then she said, "You're a most unusual woman, Nikki-the-Warrior, but I feel like I can learn a thing or two from you."

"Happy to help, General."

# CHAPTER 5

Livvy and Kevin flew ahead of the questers, the Princess, and her bodyguards, looking for any sign of Bethany and her kidnappers. They remained within sight of each other, but they flew separately to cover more ground.

When Kevin flew over the tavern, he looked for the watchers he had seen earlier. They all seemed to have vanished.

*"The men watching the tavern have gone,"* he said to Livvy with his mind.

*"Do you think they're with Bethany's kidnappers?"* Livvy asked.

*"If so, then there are now thirty men ahead of us. It's a good thing we have Angélique's soldiers traveling with us. Thirty to eight isn't great odds, even with a sorceress and four talented warriors."*

*"Very talented warriors,"* Livvy corrected him. *"You, Peter, Justin, and Nikki are four fighters I'd bet on against*

*any opposition. But you're right. There are too many of them. We'd better find them so we can figure out how to get Bethany back."*

*"Right."*

Kevin and Livvy flew north along the river for another ten minutes before spotting a large group of riders carrying torches.

*"Is that them?"* Livvy asked.

Kevin moved alongside the riders to get a better look. He saw Bethany in the center. *"I see Bethany,"* he said to Livvy. *"She's in the middle, and it doesn't look like they've tied her hands or harmed her in any way."*

*"Don't fly too close,"* Livvy cautioned. *"I'm going to reach out to Bethany and see what she can tell us."*

*"Bethany, it's Livvy. Can you hear me?"*

Bethany was surprised to hear Livvy's voice in her mind. She had forgotten that Livvy possessed that ability when on Annwyn.

*"I hear you, Livvy. Where are you?"*

She heard the hoot of an owl, and she resisted the urge to look up, knowing that Livvy was flying overhead.

*"Kevin's with me up here,"* Livvy said. *"Thomas is fine. He made it back to the farmhouse, and the others are taking him to the tavern before following after us. What's the situation?"*

*"They intercepted us halfway between the farmhouse and the tavern,"* Bethany replied. *"They said they're taking me to the High Kingdom because Telise has a bounty on me. My kidnappers are the Viscount's loyal soldiers, but*

*now they're working for Telise's spymaster. They were present when we killed the Viscount and destroyed his castle. They recognized Justin and you, so they know that you're the people who put them out of a job. The good news is: they never saw Nikki, Allison, or Peter leave the tavern. The bad news is: they want revenge, so don't be surprised if they try to ambush you along the way. Plus, Telise has a price on the head of any questers who've been interfering with her plans, and that's all of us. It's going to be rough getting to the Portal of Cockaigne. Oh, and the thugs don't seem to know that the portal was moved a month ago. You might be able to use that."*

*"Right. I'll tell the others. Talk soon."*

Bethany glanced up and saw the two owls flying above her. She felt better just knowing that they were there.

Nikki saw the moon appear over the mountains in the distance, and she was grateful for the light. She didn't like the idea of bumping into Bethany's kidnappers with lit torches giving away their position.

*"Nikki, can you hear me? It's Livvy."*

*"I hear you, Livvy. Did you find her?"*

*"Yes, and she's fine. The kidnappers are about thirty minutes north of the tavern, and they're taking her to the High Kingdom and Princess Telise. They're heading for the portal in Cockaigne, but they don't know that it was moved last month. They're Viscount Ladrach's men, and they were there when we killed him and destroyed his castle. They recognized Justin and me, but they didn't see you, Peter, or Allison. There's a price on our heads*

*because we've been interfering with Princess Telise's plans, plus the Viscount's former soldiers want us dead. We're not going to get a very warm reception from these guys. By the way, there are thirty of them now. The ten they left behind to watch the tavern are now traveling with them. Bethany says not to be surprised if they try to ambush us along the way."*

*"Got it. When the moon rose, we were able to ride faster. We just dropped Thomas off at the tavern, so we're at least thirty minutes away. How fast are they riding?"*

*"Full gallop, at the moment. I expect them to keep up that pace until sunrise, which is in a couple of hours."*

*"Are the two of you going to stay with them?"* Nikki asked.

*"Yes. We'll remain as owls until sunrise, and then we'll change into a variety of birds so they won't know we're following them. I'll let you know if we see them setting any traps or ambushes."*

*"Are you sure you can fly for that long?"* Nikki asked. *"I remember when you turned me into a hawk, and it was exhausting after a couple of hours."*

*"We'll take breaks along the way,"* Livvy assured her. *"They can't get too far ahead of us. Don't worry."*

*"Okay, but don't take any chances. You're our only sorcerer, and we'll need your powers before this is over."*

*"Right,"* Livvy acknowledged. *"Talk soon."*

Nikki informed the others what Livvy had told her.

"And the sorceress can speak to you... in your mind?" Angélique asked. "At this distance? And she can turn herself and Kevin into a variety of birds to follow the kidnappers at night and in the daylight?"

Nikki nodded.

"Astounding. I've never met a sorcerer or sorceress before. Are there limits to her powers?"

Nikki hesitated before answering. "Yes. Livvy has two different sets of... things she can do. Some are abilities, like being able to shapeshift, and she has no limits on that. Some are powers, like being able to change someone else's shape or creating a shield wall around us that an enemy cannot penetrate, and she can exhaust those powers. They'll recharge over time, but there are limits."

Angélique nodded. "So magical beings are not omnipotent?"

"Not that I've seen," Nikki replied. "Wizards are only as powerful as the spells they've learned, sorcerers can exhaust their powers if they're not careful... the closest I've heard of omnipotent beings here are the ones who built the master portal eons ago."

"What about where you live?" Angélique asked.

Nikki smiled. "It's probably best if I don't talk too much about where we live, General. It would be too difficult to explain, and I don't think you'd believe me."

"Why would any place on Annwyn be too difficult to explain?" Angélique sounded baffled.

Nikki glanced at the General. "Let's just say that the farther you get from the High Kingdom, the more different things can be."

Angélique snorted. "You're really not gonna tell me?"

"I think that's something you should discuss with the Grand Master," Nikki answered. "He can explain it much better than I can."

They rode on in silence as the sky on the eastern horizon began to show the first faint orange glow of sunrise.

Livvy saw the sunrise approaching. She landed in a tree ahead of Bethany and her kidnappers so she could rest and change shape. Kevin landed on the branch next to her a minute later.

As the kidnappers rode underneath them, Livvy did a quick count. Confused, she counted again.

*"Kevin, how many men were with Bethany when we first found them?"*

*"Thirty."*

*"How many do you count now?"*

Kevin looked down at the riders, who had slowed their horses to a walk.

*"Twenty-five."*

*"Me, too. So where did the other five go?"*

*"We'd have seen them if they rode ahead,"* Kevin insisted. *"They must have stopped behind us. Maybe they're watching to see if they're being followed."*

Livvy thought about this. *"We're still at least three days from the ford that takes us to the ruins of the old King's castle in Cockaigne, as I remember from the last time we were here, right?"*

*"That's the way I remember it,"* Kevin said. *"Although the river seems down a bit, so if you want the team to cross over sooner and set up an ambush at the ruins, that might not be a bad idea."*

*"I think that's something Nikki, Justin, and the General should discuss. In the meantime, we need to find those five missing thugs."*

Livvy let Nikki know that five of the kidnappers were

missing and may have been left along the way to watch for pursuit. Livvy also let Nikki know that the river was lower than it was before, and if they wanted to cross over to the west bank and try to get to the ruins of the old King's castle first, it might be worth the try.

After Nikki promised to pass along the information, Livvy transformed herself and Kevin into hawks so they could keep an eye on the kidnappers and find the five missing men.

Princess Angélique's bodyguards were divided into three groups. Eight were riding a mile ahead of the Princess and the questers. Nine were riding a mile behind the Princess and the questers.

The captain of the guard and two of the soldiers were riding with the Princess and the questers. As much as the captain had argued that the three groups should be closer together, the front and rear groups had orders to fall back around the Princess at the first sign of trouble.

Now that the sun had risen, the captain of the guard was having considerable difficulty realizing that the woman riding behind him was, in fact, his commanding General. Her altered appearance, compliments of Livvy's sorcery, made her look like an ordinary villager, rather than the rightful High Queen of the Eight Realms.

But the disbursement of his soldiers and the General's new appearance weren't the only two things he was wrestling with. He listened to every word of the Grand Master's message that Bethany had delivered to the General, and he was disturbed by the references to the army as an instrument of tyranny, rather than a peacekeeping force. He had always viewed his actions in the realms as maintaining the peace of the Eight Realms, not imposing the will of the King, but as he tried to put himself in the shoes of the people in the realms, he could see how it might appear that he and his soldiers were not being used to keep the peace.

He had to look at all of his campaigns through a different filter, and he didn't like what he saw.

He glanced at Angélique, and thought, *"The General is not like her sister or the previous Kings who ruled in my lifetime. If anyone can restore and repair the relationship between the High Kingdom and the realms, it's her. She must be protected at all costs."*

He continued riding and wrestling with his thoughts.

When Justin called for a break to water the horses, Nikki relayed the most recent information that Livvy had reported.

"So you're suggesting that we ford the river as soon as we can and attempt to reach the ruins of King Diarmaid's castle before the kidnappers?" the captain asked Nikki.

"It's something we should discuss," Nikki replied.

The captain nodded, then asked, "Are you sure the kidnappers think the Portal of Cockaigne is still near the castle?"

"According to Bethany, her kidnappers have no idea that the portal was moved closer to King Rigderg's castle, which is several days northeast of King Diarmaid's castle."

Angélique looked at Nikki. "What do you think?"

"The kidnappers are operating in their home territory, General," Nikki said after a moment. "They know this land better than we do. When we were here before, we found out the hard way that there are a number of good places for an ambush between here and the ford leading to King Diarmaid's castle. I'd like to bypass those places, rather than fight there again. If we can get to King Diarmaid's castle first, we should be able to rescue Bethany and put another kink in Telise's plans. Plus it'll reduce the number of people interfering with *our* plans."

The captain looked at Angélique. "If we go ahead and ford the river, do we cross the entire force, or do we keep some of them on this side?"

Angélique thought about it for a minute. "As much as I'd like the forward unit to put pressure on the kidnappers and mask our true intentions, if the kidnappers turn and fight, we could lose those men. I say we take the entire force across the river, and if you want to redistribute the men once we're over there, then you may do so."

Angelique looked at the questers. "Are we in agreement?"

Justin and Nikki looked at each other and nodded. "Yes, General," Nikki said.

"Send riders to the forward unit and the rear unit, and tell them to ford the river as soon as they find a safe place to cross," Angélique said to her captain.

"Yes, General."

Nikki looked at Justin. "The next time Livvy checks in, I want her and Kevin to come back. We need our sorceress with us, now that we're entering Cockaigne."

"I agree," Justin said. "And, by the way, I think you're doing a great job leading the team."

Nikki smiled. "I still see us both leading the team, but I do have a rapport building with the General."

"Exactly," Justin said. "She trusts you. So do I. Keep doing what you think is right, and I'll chime in if I feel it's necessary."

"You don't mind?"

Justin smiled, and Nikki felt her heart skip a beat. "Never," he assured her. "You're a soldier, and the General is a soldier. It's better for all of us if she's dealing with someone who understands military matters. That's not me, that's you."

Nikki leaned up and gave Justin a kiss on the cheek. "I keep forgetting how selfless you are. Thanks."

"Anytime, Nichole," he whispered.

Nikki's heart skipped again.

Two hours later, the soldiers and the questers were on the west bank of the river, riding north.

*"Nikki, it's Livvy. Can you hear me?"*

*"I hear you,"* Nikki replied.

*"We see you on the west bank. Five more of the kidnappers have disappeared, making ten altogether that we can't find. We don't know where they are."*

*"Thanks for the warning,"* Nikki said. *"I think it's time for you and Kevin to come back. We need you here, now that we're entering Cockaigne. If you want, you can send Kevin back up to watch Bethany and the kidnappers, but you should be here."*

Nikki didn't hear anything for a minute. Then she heard Livvy say, *"Okay. I'll come back. Kevin wants to stay here until sundown. Then I'll transform him into an owl to watch them after it gets dark. With the way their men are disappearing, we're not comfortable leaving them unobserved any longer than necessary."*

*"Okay. See you soon."*

Nikki relayed Livvy's information to the others.

Less than ten minutes later, Nikki heard the cry of a hawk overhead. It circled the group and then landed on Livvy's horse. A moment later, the hawk transformed into Livvy.

"Welcome back," Nikki said pleasantly.

Running alongside the west bank of the river were a series of hills. The ten men who had disappeared from the kidnappers, including the sergeant, watched the questers from the top of one of those hills. They weren't close enough to hear anything, but they could see everything.

"Those soldiers are from the Army of the High Kingdom," one of the men said.

"I know," the sergeant said. "But Princess Angélique isn't with them. They must searching for the Princess and her army. They're no concern of ours."

The sergeant pointed to the questers. "But those folks... they *are* a concern of ours. I recognize three of them. They're the ones who killed the Viscount and destroyed his castle. We have a score to settle with them."

"What do you want to do?" one of his men asked. "If we attack them, we outnumber them ten to nine. Not great odds, but we could try."

The sergeant thought about it for a moment. "I'd like

to know what they're doing here before I kill them. When they stop for the night, we'll grab one of them for interrogation. Once we know what they're doing, then we can kill them."

"Which one do we grab?" the man asked.

The sergeant pointed to Livvy. "Not the sorceress. She could kill us all before we had her hands tied. No, we need to plan her demise carefully." He pointed to Justin and Nikki. "One of them two should do nicely."

Shortly before sundown, Kevin reported that Bethany and her kidnappers had stopped for the night. He was perched in a nearby tree, and as soon as the sun had set behind the western hills, Kevin transformed into an owl. With the keen eyesight of the night hunter, Kevin watched the campsite from his perch, giving him time to rest from all the flying he had been doing.

Angélique's soldiers continued forward until it was too dark to see. The forward unit had managed to get past the kidnappers, as had the questers. The rear unit was even with the kidnappers when they stopped for the night.

The three units opted to maintain a cold camp, so the kidnappers wouldn't see them across the river.

"I'll take the first watch," Justin offered once the questers had seen to their horses and were preparing to go to sleep.

"And I'll take the second watch," Peter offered.

"Do you want some company?" Nikki asked Justin with a wink.

Justin smiled. "As enticing as that sounds, you've had a big day. Get some sleep, and I'll join you when Peter relieves me."

Nikki nodded, gave him a kiss, and laid down on her bedroll. Her sword, bow, and quivers were next to her within easy reach.

Angélique saw this and asked, "Are you expecting trouble?"

"When I'm here, I always expect trouble," Nikki said. "'Fortune favors the prepared mind,' and I like to stay prepared for anything when I'm anywhere near the late-Viscount's men."

Nikki pulled her traveling cloak up around her neck to ward off the cold air. Then she closed her eyes and fell asleep.

The sergeant and his men watched the camp for an hour, making sure everyone except for Justin was asleep. Then they crept toward the camp.

Justin was sitting on a rock with his back to the hills, so he could watch the camp and the river beyond. He never expected that the men Kevin and Livvy had lost were on the west bank of the river.

The sergeant and his tracker moved forward silently while the rest of the men waited halfway up the hillside. When the sergeant and the tracker were a few feet behind Justin, the tracker hefted the club that he had been carrying. He took two steps forward and swung the club. It

connected with Justin's head, and the sergeant ran forward to grab Justin before he hit the ground.

Justin was disarmed, bound, and gagged quickly, and then the sergeant and the tracker half carried and half dragged him up the hill, where the rest of the men were waiting, leaving Justin's weapons behind.

The men carried Justin to the top of the hill. Their horses were still at their campsite, just behind the crest of an adjacent hill, and the men made their way in that direction. The moon was rising, and its cold blue light helped the men see where they were going.

Once they arrived at their camp, they added wood to the fire to get warm, and then they strapped Justin down to a squarish rock that looked like an executioner's block, so he was kneeling with his arms around the rock and his head hanging off the rock's edge.

The sergeant removed Justin's gag and splashed water in his face. Justin sputtered as he regained consciousness. He struggled against his bonds, and then he gave up.

"Good. You're awake," the sergeant taunted Justin. "Now you're going to answer some questions for us. If you tell us what we want to know, you might just live through the night."

# CHAPTER 6

Nikki woke up from a light sleep. She glanced toward Justin, just in time to see two men grab him and tie him up. Then the two men hauled Justin up the hill.

She carefully stood and fastened her cloak around her neck. She procured her weapons and headed after the men. She saw Justin's weapons next to the rock where he had been sitting. She grabbed his sword and started climbing the hill.

She tried to move as quietly as she could in the moonlight, and none of the men who had taken Justin seemed to notice that she was following them.

When the men reached their campsite, Nikki hid behind a large tree. She felt the warmth from their fire as they added wood to it, but the tree kept her hidden in the shadows.

She watched as the men tied Justin to the squarish rock. *"That looks like an executioner's block. There's no way they're going to harm Justin. Not while I'm alive."*

"What do you want with me?" Justin demanded.

The sergeant and his men laughed. "Think we answer to you, do ya? Nah, we're asking the questions. You give the answers. If we like the answers, you live. If we don't like the answers, you die, and then the rest of your companions die. Yeah, we know you're the bunch that killed the Viscount and put us all out of a job. But we got a new job, see? We'll earn three year's wages for the redhead we snagged. You? Hell, we'll do you for free, even though Princess Telise wants you, too. Maybe we'll give her the warrior girl and the others, but you and the sorceress... well, that all depends on what you tell us, got it?"

Justin spat. "Ask your questions."

The sergeant laughed again, but it was a cold laugh, and Justin felt a shiver go up his spine.

The first questions he was asked were innocent enough. What was he doing there? Why was he following the kidnappers? Did he expect to be able to rescue the redhead? Why did he kill the Viscount?

When asked the last question, Justin responded, "What makes you think I killed the Viscount?"

"Because we saw you there when he was killed," the sergeant roared. "You think any of us will ever forget that day?"

"So, you saw *me* kill him?" Justin pressed.

"No, but we know it was you and your companions," the sergeant replied.

"You don't know anything," Justin said with as much

contempt as he could put into his voice. "You saw me near the castle, the castle was destroyed, so I must have been part of destroying the castle? What a load of nonsense. I was there to recover some stolen items, and nothing more. I did recover those items, and then I left and returned them to the proper owners."

"So you admit you were inside the castle," the sergeant accused.

"Yes, and it was still standing when I went inside and when I left it."

The sergeant turned to talk quietly with his men.

Justin looked at them. *"They're going to kill me, no matter what I say. Then they're going to kill everyone else. If they end up killing Angélique, she'll return to her real form as soon as she's dead. These thugs will be rewarded beyond imagining, if they can make it through the portal before her soldiers kill them."*

Justin thought about Nikki—her smile, the way she tucked her hair behind her ear, her curves, the way she made love to him, the way she made him feel every day they were together, the way she made him feel like the luckiest man alive... *"God, I hope I didn't convince her to come with me to Annwyn just to get her killed. After what happened last time we were here, I had no right to bring her along on this quest, and frankly, neither did Thor and Bethany. I can't be the cause of her death, but what can I tell these fools that will keep her alive? How can I get free and warn the others? I'm probably going to die on this hill, and Nikki will probably die on the banks of the river below. I finally find the love of my life, and this is how the story ends? I can't believe it."*

The sergeant turned back toward Justin. "If you didn't

kill the Viscount, who did?"

"The sorcerer," Justin replied.

"You mean the sorceress? The woman at your camp?"

"No," Justin replied. "The sorcerer. *He* killed the Viscount and brought down the castle."

"Where is this sorcerer?" the sergeant demanded.

"He didn't come on this job," Justin said. "He's guarding something that Princess Telise wants, and it's his job to make certain that she never gets it. I don't know where he is."

"I think you're lying," the sergeant growled.

"Then why don't you prove it," Justin retorted.

"This is a waste of time," the tracker said to the sergeant. "Let's kill him and go down and grab another member of the group."

The sergeant nodded. "Yeah. Grab the warrior girl. Maybe she'll talk when she sees what we did to this fool."

The tracker drew his sword and walked toward Justin. "I haven't sharpened my sword in a while, so it may take more than one whack to remove your head. Hope it doesn't hurt *too* much."

The tracker and the other men laughed. The tracker raised his sword.

Justin closed his eyes, waiting for the blow that would end his life.

He heard a faint whistling sound, and he was convinced that it was the sword blade swinging down at him. But no blow came. Justin opened his eyes, and he saw the arrow protruding from the tracker's chest.

"Hurry up," the sergeant said.

The tracker stood frozen for a moment, and then he sank to his knees and fell over, dead.

"What—?"

Justin heard the whistling sound again, and he knew that one of the other questers must be nearby.

The thug next to the sergeant fell to the ground.

The sergeant drew his sword and ran at Justin.

He didn't make it. An arrow pierced his neck, severing his brain stem. He fell and struck his head on the side of the stone. His head bounced off the stone as his lifeless body hit the ground.

Pandemonium broke out as the others realized what was going on. Three men were dead already, and three more died quickly after that.

With only four men remaining, all thoughts of Justin left them as they ran for their horses, only to find that the horses and been untied from their tether line and were gone.

Then they heard the shriek of an infuriated woman, sending shivers up their spines.

Justin laughed as he saw Nikki, a sword in each hand, step into the light and storm toward the survivors with all the fury a woman could muster when her lover was in danger.

She swung both swords, and two heads toppled to the ground, right before their bodies fell. The two remaining survivors tried to draw their swords, but Nikki was too fast... and too enraged. Her swords flashed and decapitated one of the two in a flash of steel.

The last of the Viscount's men turned and ran toward Justin. He managed to draw his sword and was about to swing the blade at Justin's exposed neck, but suddenly he stopped, and his back arched, as the sword blade tore through his chest. He fell, inches away from the executioner's rock.

He was still alive when Nikki, who had thrown the sword from the other side of the campfire, reached him. She placed one foot on his back and yanked the sword out of his chest.

The last of the Viscount's men drew one final breath and then died as his chest filled with blood.

Justin looked at Nikki and smiled. "I can't believe you're here. How—?"

Nikki stuck Justin's sword into the ground and drew her dagger. She cut his bonds, sheathed the dagger, and helped him up.

Justin embraced Nikki and kissed her. He was shaking slightly from the ordeal.

Nikki pulled back and stared into his eyes. "We protect each other, remember? I was in danger before, and you came for me. You were in danger this time, and I came for you. I will always come for you. No one is going to hurt you while there's still a breath in my body."

Justin stared into her eyes, and then he kissed her again. "I love you," he whispered. "Thank you for rescuing me."

"Always," she whispered back. "I love you, too."

When they finally pulled away from each other, Nikki said, "Why don't we drag these losers into the campfire and then get back to the others. Peter probably raised the alarm when he found us missing."

Nikki handed Justin his sword, and then the two dragged the Viscount's men to the fire. The stench of burning flesh filled the hilltop. Nikki retrieved her bow and quivers, then she and Justin headed down the hill as quickly as they could, leaving the Viscount's men to burn.

Everyone was awake when Nikki and Justin returned to camp.

"Where were you?" Peter asked anxiously. "I woke up to relieve you, and you were both gone."

"Those ten kidnappers who disappeared on the other side of the river? Well, they were on this side of the river, waiting for us. They grabbed Justin for interrogation. I woke up as they were dragging him off, so I followed."

"And you didn't think to tell someone?" Livvy snapped.

"And risk losing their trail? Not a chance. And it's a good thing, too, because they were about to remove part of Justin that I happen to love very much. That's when I stepped in to prevent it."

Livvy looked at Justin, and Justin ran his finger along his neck. Livvy's eyes and mouth opened wide.

"Did you leave any survivors?" Angélique asked.

"Sorry," Nikki said. "They weren't very good fighters."

Justin relayed what questions he had been asked.

"So they recognized us as the ones who stopped Cockaigne's civil war," Livvy noted. "And Telise has a price on our heads for interfering with her plans."

"Yes, and these thugs were torn between what they could get for our capture and the enjoyment they'd get from killing us for what we did to the Viscount," Justin stated.

"Did they ever mention anything about the General?" the captain asked.

Justin shook his head. "They had no idea she's with us.

I don't think they put two-and-two together about the presence of your soldiers."

"They probably think my soldiers are looking for me, instead of protecting me," Angélique said. "That works in our favor. If they don't know I'm here, then my sister doesn't either."

"And neither does the other half of your army," Nikki said.

Angélique nodded. Then she asked, "What now?"

"I think we should break camp and head for King Diarmaid's castle," Nikki said. "There's plenty of moonlight to see by, and the sooner we get there, the longer we have to plan our ambush."

Angélique looked at her captain. "Your thoughts?"

"I agree, General. We've reduced the kidnapper's numbers by ten, giving us the superior force. Surveying the ruins and planning our ambush carefully will ensure our safety and the safety of the Grand Master's betrothed, while increasing the odds of wiping out the kidnappers entirely."

Angélique nodded. "Send riders to the forward unit and the rear unit, Captain. Tell them to break camp and head for the ruins of King Diarmaid's castle."

"Yes, General."

Livvy reached out with her mind and contacted Kevin.

*"We're on the move, Kevin,"* she said to him.

*"It's several hours before dawn,"* Kevin replied. *"Why so early?"*

*"Those ten kidnappers we lost? They were on this side*

*of the river, waiting for us. They grabbed Justin for interrogation and execution. Nikki woke up, saw them, followed them, and killed them before they could hurt Justin. When they got back to camp, it seemed a good idea to head north and try to get to the ruins before the kidnappers do."*

*"Good plan,"* Kevin noted.

*"How many kidnappers are at the camp you're watching?"* Livvy asked.

*"Holding steady at twenty, although I think their leader was one of the men who ended up on your side of the river. There's no one down there giving orders. They all act like they're obeying orders that someone else gave them. That'll make them a less effective fighting force, if your ambush plans work."*

*"That's good to know,"* Livvy said. *"Do you want to come back and be with us?"*

Kevin hesitated. *"As much as I do, someone needs to watch Bethany, and you're needed where you are. Just keep changing me from owl to hawk with the sun, and I'll keep a close watch on them. But once they ford the river, I'll head for wherever you're waiting for them. I don't want to miss a good fight."*

*"Good. I'll check in later. I love you."*

*"I love you."*

Livvy shared Kevin's information with the others. Then they continued riding north in silence as the air grew colder.

Nikki rode next to Justin as they headed north along the

river. She knew he had been through a terrible ordeal, and she wanted to be there to help him the way he had been there to help her when she needed it.

About two hours after sunrise, which was obscured by heavy clouds, Nikki reached for Justin's hand. "Are you okay?" she asked gently.

Justin nodded. "It's strange. I was sad that I was about to die, but I felt guilty that I convinced you to come back here with me. I didn't want to be responsible for your death, and I felt angry that Bethany and Thor and I put you in that position. And when the guy stepped forward and raised his sword, all I could think about was you."

Justin paused, and Nikki just continued holding his hand. "And then you roared, and I saw you step into the light. At first, I couldn't decide if you were a Valkyrie coming to take my dead body to Valhalla, or if it was really you, and I was still alive. When you started lopping heads off, I *knew* it was you. Nice shooting with your bow, by the way. When I saw the arrow sticking out of that guy's chest, I knew someone had come for me. I'm glad it was you."

"I'm just glad I woke up as they were taking you away," Nikki said. "I wasn't going to let anyone hurt you, so I followed them. The fools didn't post any guards, so they all had their back to me. It was too easy. Makes you wonder how the Viscount ever got as far as he did. He must have had a lot of help from Telise."

"Speaking of which," Justin said, "do you think we'll find more of the Viscount's former soldiers working for Telise as we go on, or do you think most of them are in Riverstone?"

"Probably in Riverstone," Nikki said. "I think the tavern owner said that the rest of Telise's spies are deployed across the realms. As long as none of them can hear what Angélique says when we meet with the Kings of the realms, then Telise shouldn't be able to find out where Angélique is hiding and what she's doing."

Justin nodded. "Just as long as no one else is looking for us. I don't want a repeat of our first quest together, having to fight every day because the Viscount's men had been warned that we were coming."

"You and me both," Nikki said.

For the next two days, the questers, Angélique, and her soldiers rode north, stopping only to rest and water the horses, and for sleep when it became too dark to see.

Nikki kept a close watch on Justin, but he seemed to be bouncing back to his old self the farther away they rode from where he had been interrogated and nearly decapitated.

Kevin kept them informed about the kidnappers. Their numbers remained steady, and they were definitely heading for the ford to cross the river near King Diarmaid's ruined castle.

Bethany seemed to be doing fine, and Livvy kept her informed about what was going on. She confirmed that the leader of the kidnappers had been one of the men who disappeared, meaning that he was one of the men who Nikki killed when she rescued Justin.

On the morning of the third day, they reached the ruins of King Diarmaid's castle. The portal had been located in what looked like a large amphitheater halfway between the castle and the nearby village, which seemed to be prospering again.

The forward unit of soldiers had already arrived and were camped on the far side of the castle. The rear unit arrived an hour after the questers and Angélique arrived.

Angelique, the captain of her guards, Nikki, Justin, and Livvy all examined the ruins and the old portal, working on an ambush strategy to rescue Bethany and deal with her kidnappers.

Late that afternoon, after reviewing several possibilities for the ambush, Livvy said, "If you're open to a bit of sorcery, I can put a shield wall around Bethany that'll keep anyone or anything from harming her. I can also provide some dragon fire, to impress upon the Viscount's other men not to interfere with the questers who killed him and destroyed his castle."

"Won't that call attention to us?" the captain asked.

"No more than soldiers from the High Kingdom participating in a skirmish in Cockaigne," Livvy pointed out. "News of that will spread just as fast as news of two dragons wiping out the Viscount's former soldiers. But no one will suspect that soldiers from the Army of the High Kingdom were here if dragons are involved, so none of Telise's spies should give it a second thought. General, if we want to keep your presence here a secret, it might be best if none of your soldiers are seen."

Angélique looked at her captain, who nodded. "She's right, General. We don't want to call attention to your presence in Cockaigne. It could make traveling to King Rigderg very difficult."

Angélique smiled. "Real dragons?"

Livvy shook her head. "No, but they'll do the job."

Livvy turned to the others. "Who wants to be dragon

number two?"

Nikki raised her hand. "I've been a bird before, so I'll do it."

"Good," Livvy said. "I'll have Kevin join us, and he can show you how to be a dragon. After all, he's been one twice before."

Nikki nodded.

Livvy contacted Kevin, who promised to meet them at the ruins within the hour. The kidnappers were about to cross the ford anyway, and Kevin told them that the kidnappers would be at the ruins first thing in the morning.

Kevin arrived at the ruins, and Livvy transformed him back into his human form.

"Are you sure you're up for this?" Kevin asked after she explained the plan to him. "You've been keeping me as a bird for days, changing me back and forth based on the sun. We need you to be strong in case something unexpected happens."

Livvy smiled. "I can do this. My powers are considerably stronger than they were last time. But I'll be careful. Changing you into a dragon will tax me, but if I do it early enough, then I'll be ready to create the shield wall around Bethany by the time the kidnappers get here. It's transforming you and Nikki into dragons in the heat of the moment that'll put too much of a strain on me."

Kevin nodded. "If the only use of your power is to change us into dragons, and not keep us in the form of dragons, why don't you go ahead and transform us? That'll give me time to train Nikki on how to be a dragon, and then we can hide in the ruins and wait for the kidnappers to arrive."

Livvy turned to Nikki, who was standing nearby. "What do you think?"

"Why not?" Nikki asked. "It'll be good to get in some practice before I have to go into combat."

Livvy asked Justin to lead the horses away, and then she asked the others to move back. Once everyone had cleared the area, Livvy concentrated, and where Nikki and Kevin had stood, there were two dragons.

Kevin was his usual red dragon, but Nikki was a green dragon. Livvy created a way for Kevin and Nikki to communicate directly with each other, so she wouldn't have to relay messages between them. It was the first time she had attempted anything like that before, but it worked.

Kevin spent the next hour teaching Nikki how to fly as a dragon, and how to shoot fire from her mouth. They practiced well away from the river and from the village, so they wouldn't be seen.

Once Nikki understood how to be a dragon, and she and Kevin had worked out the battle plan, they returned to the castle ruins to wait and watch.

The soldiers standing watch along the edge of the ruins spotted the kidnappers approaching shortly after dawn the next morning. Bethany's red hair was impossible to miss in the morning sun.

The soldiers climbed down from the walls and redeployed behind the castle so they wouldn't be seen.

Angélique wanted to watch the battle, but she was convinced to remain with her soldiers, just in case something went wrong with the plan. The questers were inside the castle, near the main gates. Livvy was there to create the shield wall around Bethany. The rest were there to protect Livvy.

When the kidnappers were close enough, Livvy created the shield wall. Bethany knew the plan, and when she felt the shield all around her, she knew that the trap was about to be sprung.

Livvy raised her arms, and Kevin and Nikki extended their wings and slowly rose into the air.

When the kidnappers saw two dragons rise from the ruins of the castle, they panicked. Two of the kidnappers tried to grab Bethany and pull her away from the castle, but the shield wall prevented them.

The dragons rose higher, making them visible to the nearby villagers.

The kidnappers abandoned Bethany and tried to turn and gallop back to the river, but Kevin flew past them and turned to block their path. Nikki was behind them.

The kidnappers were alone and caught between two dragons.

Bethany rode to the castle gates to be with the others. Once she was safe, Kevin signaled Nikki, and they both shot fire from their mouths, incinerating the kidnappers in an instant. Some of the kidnappers tried to escape, but Kevin and Nikki dealt with them until none remained.

Kevin and Nikki flew off to the south. As soon as they landed on the ground, they transformed back into their human forms.

Nikki grinned at Kevin. "That was awesome!"

"A fitting end to their miserable lives," Kevin said.

They walked a short distance to a grove of trees, where their horses were waiting for them. Two of Princess Angélique's soldiers had hidden the horses in the grove the previous evening, allowing Kevin and Nikki to transform into their human forms far away from the villagers who witnessed the dragon attack.

As far as the people in the village were concerned, this was an attack by two real dragons with no sorcery involved.

Nikki and Kevin checked their mounts, and a few minutes later, they were riding north toward the ruins of King Diarmaid's castle to rejoin the others.

# CHAPTER 7

Bethany, the questers, Princess Angélique, and her soldiers rode east and forded the river before turning northeast toward King Rigderg's castle.

"I don't suppose you'll need me for your meeting with the King," Bethany said to Livvy.

"I don't think so," Livvy replied. "It's Nikki, Kevin, and me that he'll remember from our first quest, so we're the ones who need to make the introductions for Angélique."

Bethany nodded. "Then if you don't mind, can we head for the portal first? I'd like to get back to Alesia as soon as I can. Thor is probably worried out of his mind by now."

"Sure. Where is the new portal?"

"Just south of Rigderg's castle, near the road that goes toward the village," Bethany replied.

"It's on our way, so that should be fine," Livvy said.

"What are we going to do with the General's soldiers?" Nikki asked later when they stopped to water and rest the horses. "If we're trying to keep her presence here a secret, won't they alert everyone in the area that she's here in Cockaigne?"

"I've been thinking about that," Angélique replied. "We can do one of two things. First, we send all of the soldiers to see King Rigderg, arriving the day before the rest of us do. They can ask if the King has seen me or my army, and when he says that he hasn't, then they can ride off and wait at a rendezvous point for us to rejoin them once we've met with the King."

"I'm not comfortable with the bulk of your bodyguards being so far away from us," the captain of the guards stated.

"We should be able to handle anything that arises," Nikki said.

The captain seemed unconvinced. "At least allow three or four of us to remain with you," he implored.

Angélique nodded. "That seems prudent."

"Just out of curiosity," Nikki asked, "what was the second option?"

Angélique smiled. "Leave the soldiers hidden at the rendezvous point and approach the King without them. The reason I didn't like this plan as much is because the soldiers could still be discovered, and that would raise questions we don't want asked. Letting them be seen openly looking for me is a safer ploy for all concerned."

"I agree," Justin said.

Nikki agreed.

The captain still looked concerned, but he relented. "I support the first option."

"Then that's what we'll do," Angélique stated.

It was a four-day ride from the ford to King Rigderg's castle. As much as the questers and the Princess wanted to stay at the inns on the east bank of the river—for the food and the warmth—they didn't want to call attention to the group, so they bypassed the inns and camped each night. It was quite cold, but safety was the primary concern, not comfort.

On the morning of the second day after they forded the river, Angélique's soldiers formed a single unit and galloped north, so they'd arrive at King Rigderg's castle the day before Angélique and the questers arrived.

The captain of the guard accompanied the soldiers, since it would look odd if that many soldiers appeared without an officer in charge. The three bodyguards who remained with the Princess were among the best fighters and archers the captain had with him.

After the soldiers disappeared in the distance, the questers, Bethany, Angélique, and her bodyguards took a leisurely pace north.

"The last time we were in this region, we were running for our lives," Allison mentioned. "Between Ladrach's thugs and Rigderg's soldiers, I thought for sure we'd be captured or killed."

"When Livvy and Nikki and I rode to meet Lord Rigderg for the first time," Kevin commented, "Livvy had to turn me into a dragon to deal with all of Ladrach's soldiers who tried to intercept us."

"I'm glad this is a more pleasant journey than our last time here," Nikki said.

"It's a pity your first adventure in Cockaigne had to be so perilous," Angélique said. "This realm has the reputation of being peaceful and prosperous. I had no idea that a civil war was brewing. I guess my sister kept that from me, so I wouldn't send soldiers here to enforce the peace. At least you were able to thwart her plans."

Two hours after sunrise on the fourth day of their journey, the spires and pennants of King Rigderg's castle became visible over the treetops.

"We should be there within the next thirty minutes," Nikki estimated.

"Don't forget, we're going to the portal first," Bethany reminded everyone.

"I haven't forgotten," Nikki confirmed. "Although I wish you were staying with us. I've missed you since you..." Nikki had to be careful not to reveal too much to Angélique. "...went to live with Thor, and we haven't really spent much time together on this quest."

"We'll see each other soon," Bethany said. "After all, the council of the Kings will be at Thor's residence."

As they approached the castle, they could see quite a bit of expansion underway. Additional foundations had been laid, and stones were being stacked to form walls for the new interior buildings. Even the village looked like it was growing.

"Now that the portal is here, this is the center of commerce for Cockaigne," Bethany explained when Kevin pointed out the changes. "The King needs more space for his ministers, and the village needs more space to receive goods from and transport goods to the other realms."

As they approached the portal, Livvy recognized the

location immediately. It was next to the two hills where Ladrach's soldiers tried to capture her before she could meet with Lord Rigderg. It was an ideal location, even if it did hold some unpleasant memories for her.

Several soldiers, wearing the King's emblem on their uniforms, were guarding the portal. They all had swords, but several were also carrying crossbows. The Portal Keeper, who lived in the stone house next to the portal, was nowhere to be seen.

"State your business here," one of the soldiers demanded as they approached.

"I need the Portal Keeper to send me to Alesia," Bethany replied. "I am the Grand Master's betrothed, and the Portal Keeper knows me."

A couple of the guards looked at each other. "That's her all right. Grab her and kill the others!"

Angélique's bodyguard moved between her and the guards. Nikki, Justin, and Peter drew their swords and attacked the guards. Kevin held back in reserve, so he could protect Livvy and Allison.

Several of the guards fell as Nikki, Justin, and Peter's swords flashed in the morning sunlight. One of the guards aimed his crossbow at Justin, but Nikki reared her horse, and its front hooves kicked out, turning the guard's face into a bloody mass. The guard fell, twitching, as he died from his wounds.

Another guard aimed his crossbow at Livvy. Kevin leaped from his saddle and grabbed Livvy, pushing her off her horse. The crossbow bolt struck the backplate of his armor, ricocheted off, and struck Allison in the chest.

Allison looked down at the bolt with a confused look on her face. Then her body sagged as she slid off her horse.

"Allison!" Peter screamed.

Kevin looked over at Allison in horror. Bethany had already dismounted and was running for Allison's body, which was sprawled on the ground. Kevin helped Livvy to her feet, and she quickly joined Bethany.

Peter, Nikki, and Justin viciously finished off the remaining guards. None survived. After making certain that no more guards were hiding nearby, Peter raced back to be with Allison while Nikki and Justin searched for the Portal Keeper.

"Is she going to be all right?" Peter implored when he reached Allison.

"Get back," Bethany snapped. "I'm still trying to see how bad the damage is."

Livvy could tell that Allison wasn't breathing. She put Allison's body in stasis, like she did when Nikki had been badly injured.

Bethany looked at Livvy. "She's gone," she whispered.

"No!" Peter cried. "You have to do something."

Livvy knew what she needed to do, but Allison's body had to be repaired first. She couldn't resurrect someone into a broken body. She concentrated on the wound, mentally exploring the torn and damaged tissue.

"Remove the bolt, Bethany," Livvy said calmly. She felt anything but calm, but she kept her voice steady to reassure the others. She had never attempted what she was about to do, but she had to try anyway.

Bethany obeyed and pulled out the bolt.

"Now focus, Bethany. You're a trauma nurse. You know what the heart and the surrounding area is supposed to look like when it's healthy and uninjured. Concentrate on that. I need to see what you see when you're looking at an undamaged chest cavity."

Bethany complied, and Livvy looked into Bethany's thoughts. Livvy saw what a pristine chest cavity looked like, and she compared it to Allison's. Then she began repairing Allison's heart and the other damaged tissue around it. Her fractured rib was fused back together, the heart muscle was knitted back together and healed, blood vessels were repaired and sealed against leaks... all at blinding speeds.

"What about the blood in the chest cavity?" Livvy asked Bethany.

"It needs to be put back into the heart and blood vessels," she replied.

Livvy returned the blood to the blood vessels. She looked into Bethany's mind again and compared it with Allison's chest cavity. Satisfied that she had repaired the damage, Livvy removed the entry wound in Allison's chest and the hole in her dress. Then she motioned for everyone to stand back.

Bethany stood and grabbed Peter's arm, pulling him away. The others formed a ring around Livvy and Allison, watching and waiting.

Livvy concentrated, not understanding what she was doing, but confident that she was doing what needed to be done. She was surrounded by darkness—impenetrable blackness everywhere she looked. But in the distance, she saw a faint glow. Her mind moved toward it, and she saw Allison. She was dressed as she had been before the attack, and her body glowed.

Livvy tried to pick up Allison, but she was too heavy. Livvy tried again, and she noticed that the glow from Allison's body was growing fainter. Somehow, she knew she didn't have much time.

"What do I do?" Livvy cried out in her mind.

"Summon the light." The answer seemed to come from all around her. The voice was majestic and loving, and Livvy couldn't tell if it were male or female, but it strengthened her.

Livvy focused all of her powers. "I summon the light!"

A pillar of pure white light dropped down from above. It seemed to come from nowhere and from a tremendous distance all at the same time. The light shone on Allison, and her body began glowing brighter.

When Allison was glowing almost as brightly as the light itself, Livvy heard the voice say, "Step into the light and pick her up."

Livvy obeyed, and she found Allison to be light as air in her arms.

"Remain in the light, and I will lead you back. She will remember nothing of what has happened, and it is for the best that it remains that way."

A moment later, Livvy was on her knees, next to Allison's body. She placed the Allison in her arms onto Allison's body, and the two became one again.

The others only saw Livvy's arms move like they were lifting something and then putting it back down. Only Livvy saw Allison's spirit in her arms.

Livvy was exhausted. She had never attempted a resurrection before, and she now understood why the tavern owner had said it might take two sorcerers to do it. That she did it by herself was remarkable. That she was still conscious after the strain was a miracle.

As much as she wanted to rest, she needed to finish bringing Allison back to life. She wiped the sweat off her face and concentrated. First, Livvy started Allison's heart, checking for leaks or any part of the heart muscle not working properly. Everything seemed to be functioning normally.

Livvy then willed Allison to breathe, and Allison's chest rose and lowered as she began breathing normally. Livvy stayed in control until she was certain that Allison was alive. Then she let go of everything except Allison's mind, keeping her unconscious for a minute longer.

"Is she okay?" Tears streamed down Peter's cheeks.

Livvy nodded. "She won't remember anything that happened," Livvy said with difficulty, "and that's for the best. All she needs to know is that she fell off her horse. Nothing else." Livvy looked into the eyes of everyone surrounding her. "Your word on this—you will never tell her what happened. She fell off her horse. That's all."

Everyone nodded.

Then Livvy looked at Peter. "Dry your eyes, Peter. I'm not waking her up until you're composed."

Peter complied, wiping his eyes with his sleeve.

Kevin, realizing how tired Livvy was, brought her one of the waterskins so she could drink. Then he handed her a quarter of an apple and some dried meat. She wolfed it down, drank more water, and handed the waterskin back to Kevin with a grateful smile. "Thanks for that," she said.

"Someday, you'll have to tell me what you just did," he whispered.

Livvy nodded. Then she straightened up, took a deep breath, and released Allison's mind.

Allison's eyes fluttered open. "Wha... what happened?"

Livvy helped Allison sit up. "You fell off your horse when the guards started shooting their crossbows," Livvy replied. "You must have hit your head when you landed. Bethany checked you out, and you should be fine."

"Really?" Allison asked. "I had the strangest dream. Can you dream when you're unconscious?"

"I guess anything's possible," Livvy commented.

Allison looked around. "What about the guards?"

"Dead," Peter replied. "Something tells me they were either more of Ladrach's men, or they were spies working for Telise, or both. Either way, they won't bother us again."

Peter and Livvy helped Allison to her feet and gave her a drink of water. She was about to ask a question when she heard Nikki shouting.

"We found the Portal Keeper and his assistants," Nikki said. "They were tied up in his house, but they seem okay."

Bethany ran to the Portal Keeper's house.

"Bethany!" the Portal Keeper exclaimed. "You're okay. Those men were waiting for you. Something about a reward that Princess Telise was offering. They had orders to kill anyone who brought you to the portal."

"No honor among spies," Nikki said. "The kidnappers were dead either way."

Bethany nodded. "Are you all right?" she asked the Portal Keeper. "Can you send me through the portal to Alesia?"

The Portal Keeper nodded. "It'll be my honor, Bethany. Give me a moment to get my circulation going again, and I'll send you along. Those people tied my ropes a bit tight."

As Bethany waited for the Portal Keeper to open the portal and send her home, Allison pulled Livvy aside.

"What really happened to me?"

"What do you mean?" Livvy asked.

"I remember falling off my horse, and then I was surrounded by darkness. Then you were there, and then I was surrounded by light. The next thing I knew, I was back here again."

"The mind can play tricks on you sometimes," Livvy said. "You bumped your head on the ground, your mind wandered around without you, and then you woke up. It was just a dream, like any other."

"But my head doesn't hurt," Allison protested.

Livvy smiled. "Good! Then there's nothing wrong with you. Don't let a weird dream make you anxious. You're obviously all right, so why think about anything else?"

Allison looked at Livvy suspiciously, and then she shrugged. "I guess you're right."

Angélique, who had heard Allison and Livvy talking, stared in shocked disbelief at what she had just witnessed. When Allison walked away to be with Peter, Angélique whispered, "She was dead!"

Livvy nodded.

"You brought her back from the dead!"

Again, Livvy nodded.

"How?"

"To be honest, I'm not entirely sure," Livvy admitted. "I knew what to do, but I have no idea *how* I knew. I think someone was there helping me, but I don't know who, and I don't know how."

"And yet you tried anyway."

Livvy nodded. "That's what I do for my friends."

Angélique shook her head. "It seems that you and Nikki share that particular sense of loyalty for your companions."

"That's why we get along so well. We're very much

alike, and we're also very different. But at our core, what really matters, we're the same. She has killed to protect her friends. I've killed to protect my friends, too, but killing is easy. Anyone can do it when sufficiently provoked. The true measure of a friendship isn't that you'd kill to protect one another, it's what you'd do when killing isn't an option. What would you risk for one another? That's what matters. Nikki nearly sacrificed her life for all of us. I risked all of my powers for Allison. That's the measure of our friendship."

Angélique stared at Livvy in awe. "I have seen things on this journey that I never thought existed before, and now I'm forced to reevaluate nearly everything that I ever believed—particularly about friendships and sacrifice. If we live through all this, I need to explore these concepts some more. In the meantime, I guess we should say goodbye to Bethany."

Angélique gestured toward the Portal Keeper, who had exited his house and was walking to the portal.

Bethany quickly hugged everyone goodbye, and said, "I'll see you all at the council of the Kings." She nodded to the Portal Keeper.

The Portal Keeper concentrated for a moment, and then the portal opened, revealing Alesia beyond. Bethany stepped through the portal and disappeared. The portal closed behind her.

"Is there anywhere I can send the rest of you?" the Portal Keeper asked.

"Not yet," Nikki replied. "But hopefully we'll be in need of your services soon. Tell me; is King Rigderg in his castle?"

"Yes, he's there."

"Thank you," Nikki said. "We need to meet with him, and then we'll be back."

"I'll be here," the Portal Keeper said pleasantly. "And thank you for rescuing me and dealing with these ruffians. If you could drag them away from the portal, I'd be most grateful."

Nikki, Justin, Peter, Kevin, and the three bodyguards dragged the bodies into the woods behind the portal. Once that was done, they mounted their horses and rode to King Rigderg's castle. There was still a meeting that needed to take place.

When the questers, Princess Angélique, and her bodyguards reached the top of the causeway leading to the gates of King Rigderg's castle, two guards stepped forward and blocked their path.

"State your business, please," one of the guards said.

"Would you be so kind as to inform King Rigderg that Livvy-the-Sorceress and Nikki-the-Warrior wish to pay their respects and have a private audience, if he's not too busy at the moment," Livvy replied.

The guard's face showed recognition, and he smiled broadly. "My ladies, I recognize you from the last time you were here. I'll send someone to inform the King of your arrival. I'm certain he'll be delighted to receive you."

The guard shouted orders that the King be informed immediately. Then he noticed that several in the party had blood splatter on their clothing.

"It looks like you've been in a skirmish latterly," he observed.

Livvy nodded. "We stopped at the portal to send one of our party back home, only to find it being guarded by a group of assassins. We dispatched them for you."

The guard looked concerned. "And the Portal Keeper?"

"Unharmed," Livvy assured him. "He was tied up, and we freed him. He's back at his post again."

"Thank you for that, and I'm sorry you had to experience something so unpleasant upon your return. We should show you a better time, after all you did for us."

Livvy smiled at the man. "Well, here's your chance to make it up to us. Take care of our horses, provide food and drink and a place to sleep it off, and all will be forgiven."

At that moment, the King's chamberlain reached the gates. "My ladies, the King will be delighted to meet with you and your companions at once. If you'll dismount and follow me, I'll take you directly to him."

They dismounted, and grooms from the stables took charge of their horses as they followed the chamberlain through the gates.

Angélique whispered to Livvy, "What if he's not happy to meet me?"

"Don't worry," Livvy whispered back. "We'll convince him that he wants to hear what you have to say, and that you want to hear what he has to say. As long as you listen and don't get defensive, the meeting should go well."

"And if it doesn't?"

"Then we'd better hope that Thor has a better plan."

King Rigderg seemed a bit older when they entered the great hall, but his smile was broad and genuine when he recognized Livvy, Nikki, and Kevin. And when he recognized Justin he grasped Justin by both arms.

"Convinced anyone to toss a coin for their crown lately?" the King joked warmly.

"I'm afraid you were the first and the last, your Majesty."

The King then kissed Livvy and Nikki, and he shook the hands of the others. When he reached Angélique and her bodyguards, he kissed her and shook their hands.

"I see some of your party is missing, and you've added some additional members to your group," he noted.

"Yes, your Majesty," Livvy said. "And it's these newcomers that are the reason for our visit." Livvy looked around. "May we speak in private?"

The King nodded and dismissed everyone else inside the great hall. He gave orders to shut the doors and to keep anyone from disturbing him until the meeting was over.

"I hope you're not here to get me entangled in any High Kingdom business," the King said as he poured wine for everyone. "We just finished cleaning up the mess from Viscount Ladrach's attempt to cause a civil war. And then a whole platoon of High Kingdom soldiers was here yesterday, looking for Princess Angélique, as if she'd hide here in Cockaigne. With the two halves of the High Kingdom's army out there chasing after each other, Princess Angélique in hiding, Princess Telise plotting her schemes to absorb the realms into a single kingdom under her rule, and the other realms arming for war against the High Kingdom and each other, I've had my fill of intrigues and plots."

Livvy looked at Angélique and shrugged.

"So, what brings you back to Cockaigne?" the King

asked after he had handed everyone a cup of wine.

"Intrigues and plots, your Majesty," Livvy said apologetically. "Particularly involving the High Kingdom."

"You can't be serious," the King said.

"I'm afraid so, your Majesty. One member of our group represents the High Kingdom and is here to discuss options to prevent Annwyn from going up in flames."

The King's eyes narrowed. "And which of your group is this representative?"

Livvy looked at Angélique and concentrated. A moment later, Angélique was transformed into her true form.

"Your Majesty, allow me to introduce Princess Angélique, General of the Armies and the rightful Queen of the High Kingdom."

# CHAPTER 8

King Rigderg stared at Angélique with his mouth open. "Please tell me this is a joke or a trick of your sorcery," he said, taking a large gulp of his wine.

"I'm afraid not, your Majesty," Angélique said. "These good people brought me here at great peril to themselves so that you and I could speak, just as I hope to speak with the other Kings before things go so far that we cannot prevent war and the spilling of innocent blood."

The King took another gulp of wine and refilled his cup.

"Perhaps we can sit and talk?" Angélique suggested.

King Rigderg nodded and gestured for everyone to sit. Once he was seated, he said, "I hope you understand that I don't have any animosity toward you, Princess. We've lived under the tyranny of the High Kingdom for so long that we're more accustomed to being commanded to do things, rather than being asked."

"I assure you, I'm not here to command. I genuinely want to talk, and more importantly, to listen. It is clear to me that a single wrong step will destroy Annwyn altogether. I will do anything to prevent that, but I can't do it alone. I need the help of the Kings. That's why I'm here. You're the first King I'm talking to, but you won't be the last, and I hope that, once I've spoken to all of the Kings, we can convene a council of Kings at the Grand Master's residence to see what together we can do to prevent my sister from plunging us into a war no one can win."

"So you *do* recognize that the High Kingdom is at the heart of the present difficulties?" the King asked.

Angélique nodded. "I didn't, until my sister accused me of a murder that she committed. As a soldier, I've looked at the world one way. Since the false accusations were made, I've been forced to see things differently, and I'm beginning to understand just how much I don't understand, the things I've turned a blind eye to, and the mistakes I've made and my armies have made."

Angélique gestured toward the questers. "Our mutual friends here have already shown me much about friendship and sacrifice, but I have so much more to learn, and I hope you can be one of my teachers."

The King sat back and stroked his beard. Then he said, "If you're being genuine with me, then there's hope for you yet. Even though I've only been King for a few months, it's clear to me that the relationship between the realms and the High Kingdom benefits no one apart from the High Kingdom. If we're going to prevent a war, then there must be assurances that the Eight Realms will interact differently going forward. It has been hundreds and hundreds of years since the High Kingdom conquered and enslaved the realms. We have served the High Kingdom long enough. It is time for the High Kingdom to serve us."

"In what way?" Angélique inquired.

Angélique and the King talked for hours. The King eloquently stated what he thought was wrong with the way the Eight Realms were structured, the role of the High Kingdom and its armies, the excesses that Princess Telise and her late uncle were famous for, and the deep resentment that filled the realms when they thought about the High Kingdom.

After supper had been served, and the servants had retired from the great hall, the King said, "Princess, I've said things here today that I've never dared utter out loud before. If your promise that there will be no reprisals is honored, I'll count this as the most productive conversation I've ever had. And I fully support holding a council of Kings at the Grand Master's residence as soon as arrangements can be made."

"Thank you, your Majesty. And thank you for trusting me enough to share your thoughts. I have a lot to think about."

The King nodded. "So what happens next?"

"There are six more realms I need to visit," Angélique replied. "And six more Kings to convince to talk to me and meet together to resolve our differences."

"What do you need me to do?" the King asked.

"Make introductions," Angélique stated. "I don't know the Kings. I know their armies. My uncle knew the Kings, but apparently only to bully them, based on what you've shared here today. My companions only know you. I very much need you to come with me. You can make the introductions, and your presence might convince them that talking to me is a good idea."

King Rigderg's eyes bulged. He stroked his beard again, and then he poured himself another cup of wine. After he drained it, he said, "That's going to take a bit of thought. Do you mind if we discuss this again over breakfast?"

"Of course," Angélique said.

"If you don't mind," Livvy interrupted, "I need to change the Princess' appearance again, like I did when the servants entered the great hall. It's vital that no one recognizes her. Telise has spies everywhere."

The King nodded, and where Angélique had sat, there was now a woman who looked and sounded completely different.

"I'll never get used to sorcery," the King said.

"That's okay, your Majesty," Livvy said with a smile. "I don't think I'll ever get used to royalty."

The King's chamberlain assigned rooms in the guest wing for the questers, the Princess, and her bodyguards.

Allison and Peter disappeared into their room immediately, as did Livvy and Kevin. Angélique's quarters had an outer room, where her bodyguards could sleep. One remained awake at all times while the other two slept.

After checking on the others, Nikki and Justin retired to their room, which was around the corner from the others. A roaring fire was in the fireplace, giving off a warm glow as well as warmth against the cold night air.

Nikki and Justin stripped off their armor and clothing for the first time since the quest began. As they both dipped towels into the water basin next to the bed, so they could wash each other's bodies, Nikki said, "Do you realize this is the longest we've gone without being together since we first met?"

Justin nodded and he began washing her. "I've always known that there was more to our relationship than just the physical, but I've missed being intimate with you. I only feel whole when we're together, and even though I get to see you every day, it's not enough."

"For me either," Nikki said as she began washing him. "I can't count the number of times I wanted to grab you, sneak away from camp, and make love all night long, but between the soldiers, needing to rescue Bethany, and protecting the Princess, it just didn't seem possible."

Justin finished washing Nikki and allowed her to finish washing him. She spent extra time in one spot, and soon it was fully erect.

"At least we have tonight," he whispered as he took the towel from her and tossed it on the floor next to his. His hands began to explore her body, and she felt the familiar warmth radiate from her core. She reached for his erection and began stroking it. Then she sank to her knees and teased it with her tongue before placing it in her mouth so she could stimulate him orally.

It didn't take long for him to release as her lips moved forward and backward while her tongue moved around the head and the shaft.

Nikki looked up at him and said, "Wow, it *has* been a long time, hasn't it?"

Justin lifted her up and guided her toward the bed. "Too long, Nichole."

Justin sat down on the bed, but before he could do

anything, Nikki straddled him, wrapped her arms around his shoulders, and began kissing him. "You'd better hang on," she whispered. "You're in for a bumpy ride."

Justin was still fully erect. Nikki reached down to see if she was wet.

She was.

She raised herself up and guided him inside of her. With both arms around his shoulders, she began rising up and lowering herself on him.

Justin put one arm around her back to keep her from leaning too far backward and falling onto the floor, and he reached down with his other hand to stimulate her clit as she moved up and down.

Nikki's first climax was incredible. The combination of having him inside of her, along with his touch, made her stomach muscles spasm with pleasure. Even her shoulders were shaking, but she never slowed down. She continued moving up and down on his erection.

She felt his erection swell, and she knew he was about to release. She squealed with delight as she felt the hot liquid shooting inside of her. Again, she never slowed down and kept moving up and down on him, unwilling to break the connection and stop what they were sharing.

Nikki's climaxes intensified as Justin's hand continued stimulating her clit. She was climaxing so hard that she barely felt his second release inside of her. The sensation of warmth was the only indication she had that he had released again. She began moving up and down even faster than before.

Justin continued stimulating her clit, and between that, her wetness, and his cum inside of her, froth began leaking out of her and covering Justin's lap and Nikki's inner thighs.

As Justin began building toward his third release, Nikki felt an intense climax approaching. As the hot liquid shot into her, her climax hit her, and her entire body began spasming. Her arms released from his shoulders, and his arm around her back kept her from falling. Her legs shook, her stomach muscles clenched and unclenched, and her back arched as she lost all control over her body.

She felt a familiar sensation, and she broke the connection, pushed Justin onto his back, leaned forward, and squirted, sending her fluids and his cum onto the floor next to the bed.

She lay on top of him, panting with tears streaming down her face.

"Are you all right?" Justin asked, feeling the wetness against his cheeks."

"Yes," she sobbed. "It's just been so long. I needed that. I didn't realize until now how badly I needed that... how badly I need to share myself with you."

Justin took a corner of the bed sheet and wiped her tears away. "I will always be there for you, Nichole. Whatever you need, whenever you need it, for as long as I live. I swear."

Nikki leaned down and kissed him. Justin's hands roamed all over her, from her butt to her breasts, relishing the contact between his skin and her skin.

After several minutes of intimacy, Nikki rolled off of him. They washed themselves again and then cleaned up the mess they made on the floor. After that, they crawled into bed, snuggling next to each other as the fire cast its orange glow around the room.

"Are you awake enough to talk about something?"

Justin asked.

"Sure," Nikki said. "What's on your mind?"

"What happened today with Allison," he replied. "After Allison fell, and we killed the fake guards, we were looking for the Portal Keeper when Livvy... brought Allison back. But I don't know what really happened. Do you?"

"No. I know we're not supposed to tell Allison anything other than she fell off her horse and was knocked unconscious, but I don't know why that's so important. I'm going to find out, though."

"Can you fill me in when you do? I'm dying to know what really happened and how Livvy did what she did."

"Of course," Nikki promised. "I'll try to see her in the morning before breakfast. I doubt there will be time to discuss it with her after that."

Nikki woke before dawn. Justin was still sleeping soundly, so she opted not to wake him. She carefully slipped out of bed and got dressed. Instead of putting on her armor, she put on her leather doublet, wrapped her cloak around her shoulders, and went to find Livvy.

Nikki had just rounded the corner of the hallway where the others were being housed when she saw Livvy exit the room at the far end of the hall. Nikki followed her.

Livvy climbed the stairs up to the roof. Nikki caught up to Livvy as she leaned against the eastern parapet, watching the morning sky change colors as the dawn approached.

"Am I disturbing you?" Nikki asked.

"No," Livvy said tiredly. "Just watching the dawn."

"Do you mind if we talk while we watch?"

Livvy chuckled. "I can imagine what you want to talk about."

"Can you blame me?" Nikki said. "You did something that hasn't been seen on earth for nearly two thousand years, and I missed all of it. Justin and I were helping the Portal Keeper and his assistants when you... when Allison... when it happened. The only thing I know is that we're not supposed to say anything to Allison about it."

"Kevin asked me the same questions, and he was right there next to me the entire time. I guess you deserve to know, since you weren't there for any of it." Livvy turned to face Nikki. "But this is the last time I'm telling the story. You get to tell Justin and anyone else who asks, got it?"

"Got it."

Livvy began to tell the story from the beginning. When she explained why she had to repair Allison's body first, Nikki asked, "So is that why you had Thor send me through the portal after I was—"

"Yes," Livvy interrupted. "I didn't have the power to repair your body; it was too damaged. And if you had died, and I tried to bring you back, you just would've died again, and I'd never be able to bring you back."

"But you were able to repair Allison's body?"

Livvy nodded. "Her wounds weren't as bad as yours, and evidently I'm more powerful now. I can do things that I could never have done before. And don't forget, you were still alive when Thor sent you through the portal. We did that to keep you alive. Allison was already dead by the time I got to her. There was no choice but to repair her body and try to bring her back."

"And you did that by having Bethany show you in her

mind what everything should look like so you could see how Allison's body needed to be repaired?"

"Yes," Livvy said.

"Wow. That's remarkable. Thank heavens Bethany was there."

"Agreed." Livvy then told Nikki what it was like trying to bring Allison back to life.

"And this... this voice told you what to do?"

"It was like nothing I've ever heard before," Livvy admitted. "It was male, it was female, it was a fusion of the two... but it was lovely, and it brought me the peace and confidence I needed to do what had to be done."

"And in the middle of absolute darkness, with Allison's... glow fading, a pillar of white light appeared and..."

"I know it sounds crazy, but that's how I saw it. I interpreted the glow as Allison's life force, and somehow I knew that if the glow faded into darkness, I'd never be able to bring her back. The light replenished her glow, and then I was able to bring her back to her body and... rejoin the two together. After that, it was just a matter of making the body start working again—blood flowing, lungs breathing—and once her body was working on its own again, I woke her up. You know the rest."

Nikki thought about it for a moment. Then she asked, "So where was Allison when you went to get her?"

"I've been trying to figure that out ever since I saw the darkness. I don't know if it was a place, a plane of existence, a place between places, or if what I saw was just the only way my mind could process what was going on around me. All I know for sure is that Allison was dead here, her spirit was alive there, but it was fading away, and the light restored her spirit so I could bring it back to her body. Life, afterlife, light, darkness, God... I don't know how to explain these concepts, so I don't know what Allison and I really experienced. She has no memory of it, apart from flashes of memories that she thinks are dreams. As for what I saw, heard, and felt, all I can tell you is that I had help, and I was able to do something that the tavern owner told me I could do, but never explained how it was done. It's as much a mystery to me as it is to the rest of you."

Nikki put her arm around Livvy's shoulder, and Livvy reached up and took Nikki's hand in her own.

"Thank you for saving Allison," Nikki said as the rays of the morning sun broke the horizon.

"Thank you for being my best friend," Livvy said, watching the light rising over the hills in the east.

Nikki looked at Livvy and knew that her friend would never look at light the same way ever again.

At breakfast, King Rigderg presented his mother to his visitors. She recognized the questers immediately.

"We're so happy to find you well," Kevin said to her. He had been the one to find her in Viscount Ladrach's dungeons, even though it was Thor who unlocked the cell doors to free her and Duke Berngal's sister and wife.

"It is a pleasure to see all of you again," she said. "And I'm grateful to have the opportunity to thank you again for my rescue... and the rescue of my son's future wife and sister-in-law."

The King blushed at this.

"You're marrying Duke Berngal's sister?" Nikki asked.

"That's wonderful!"

"The wedding will be in the spring," the King admitted, still blushing.

After breakfast, which included enough food to feed twice as many guests, King Rigderg led the questers, Princess Angélique—still disguised—and her bodyguards back to the great hall. The doors were closed and guards posted so the King and his guests wouldn't be disturbed.

"I've given a great deal of thought about your proposal and your request, Princess," he said. "I feel duty-bound to tell you that I'm not entirely sure I trust you. There has been too much bad blood between the realms and the High Kingdom to blindly trust *anyone* from your family."

Angélique began to protest, but the King held up his hand, and she fell silent.

"That being said, you are the first representative of the High Kingdom I've ever known to listen to the grievances of the realms without retaliating or arguing. It's refreshing, and it does give me a measure of hope. Plus, I agree that any solution to our present problems can only be solved by all of the realms working together. So, for that reason, and because I trust your companions with my life, I will come with you, introduce you to the other Kings, and help you convince them to hold a council of Kings to see what we can do to stop your sister and prevent a war that will only destroy, rather than unite."

Angélique and the King stood and grasped each other's forearms.

Once they released each other, Angélique asked, "So where should we go first?"

The king reached for a map of Annwyn, which showed all of the realms, and Riverstone, but didn't include Alesia.

He spread the map out on the table and pointed to Cockaigne.

"We're here," he said, pointing to the northwest coast of the western continent. "There are two more realms on this continent: Arcadia, ruled by King Braxton, and Asphodel, ruled by King Tyrell." He then pointed to the great island between the two continents, labeled *Reingard* and *The High Kingdom*. "This is your realm, Princess. Reingard, or as you now call it, the Realm of the High Kingdom. None of your armies are there at the moment, by the way."

The King pointed to the eastern continent. "The last known sighting of the High Kingdom's army that's hunting you is here." He pointed to the realm labeled "Aaru" on the southern coast of the eastern continent. "Although that changes frequently. There seems to be no logic in their movements. One day they're in Arcadia, the next they're in Avalona on the other side of Annwyn, and then they're in Asphodel before being seen in Elysium or Brittia. They move constantly."

"How do you know where they are?" Angélique asked.

"The Portal Keeper tells me. The Grand Master instructed the Portal Keepers to let the realms know where the two armies of the High Kingdom are at all times."

Angélique drew in her breath sharply. "You know where my loyal troops are hiding?"

"Of course, Princess," the King said. "But don't worry. I haven't told anyone."

"But what about the other Kings?" she asked, concerned. "Can they be trusted with this information?"

"It's not a question of trust, Princess, it's a matter of survival," the King said. "The High Kingdom's armies are marching through the realms right now, and the realms are arming for war. The question right now is whether the realms will fight the armies of the High Kingdom, or whether they'll start fighting each other. We have to know where your armies are, and there are some Kings who don't believe that your armies have divided loyalties. They see this as just another ploy by the High Kingdom to conquer the realms."

"Is that what you believe?" Angélique asked.

The King shook his head. "No. I believe that half of the army supports you, and the other half supports your sister. I believe that *Telise* is trying to conquer the realms to create a single kingdom under her, and I believe that some of the other Kings want to take advantage of the situation for their own purposes. If you're going to convince them to band together, you're going to have to move quickly. That's why I suggest visiting Arcadia and Asphodel first. Not only are they closer, but my neighbors have very different opinions about what's going on and what should be done about it. If you can convince them, then the others will be easier to convince."

Angélique sent two of her bodyguards to the rendezvous point, where the captain of her guards and the rest of her bodyguards were hiding. Her orders were for them to ride for the portal with all possible haste, have the Portal Keeper send them to Arcadia, pretend to be searching for Angélique there, and then hide in a place that King Rigderg had suggested until it was time to go to Asphodel.

When her two bodyguards returned, she, her

bodyguards, and the questers prepared to leave Cockaigne. The King also prepared to leave, along with ten of his own bodyguards.

When asked why he was taking bodyguards with him, the King replied, “Things are uncertain in the other realms at the moment. No one has any grievances against me, but I feel more comfortable having a few swords nearby to protect me.”

From the parapet of the castle, Nikki saw the Princess’ bodyguards enter the portal. Then she descended the stairs to the great hall, where everyone was waiting.

“Your bodyguards just left for Arcadia,” she said to Angélique.

“We’ll give them an hour to make an appearance at the castle, and then we’ll follow them to Arcadia,” Angélique said. Then she looked over at the King. “If that’s all right with you, your Majesty.”

The King chuckled. “You get used to giving orders, don’t you, Princess?”

Angélique nodded. “I meant no disrespect.”

“I know,” the King said pleasantly. “Old habits die hard. I hope we can forge new ones.”

“As do I,” Angélique agreed.

An hour later, they left the castle and rode to the portal. When they dismounted the King asked the Portal Keeper, “What’s the latest on the position of the High Kingdom’s armies?”

“Princess Angélique’s army is still where it was the last time we spoke, but Princess Telise’s army is coming here tomorrow. The Portal Keeper in Aaru notified us earlier this morning.”

The King smiled. “Can you have one of your assistants

notify my mother? She'll want to be ready to receive them... properly."

The Portal Keeper laughed. "I'll see to it, your Majesty."

The King gestured toward his traveling companions. "You know who's with me?" the King whispered.

"Of course, your Majesty. The Grand Master has been keeping us well informed of her movements and those of her bodyguards. And we're watching over the questers she's traveling with, since they're the Grand Master's closest friends."

King Rigderg nodded. "We'd like to go to Arcadia now, if you don't mind."

"Not at all, your Majesty."

The Portal Keeper opened the portal. The King and his ten bodyguards entered first. Angélique and her three bodyguards entered next. The questers entered last. The Portal Keeper winked at Justin and Nikki, and then he closed the portal after they had entered and disappeared.

# CHAPTER 9

King Braxton saw the portal open and a group of twenty-one people exit into his kingdom. He had taken to watching the portal daily, waiting for the next time the Army of the High Kingdom came through to harass him and his people. Seventeen soldiers from the High Kingdom had come through the portal earlier that day, looking for Princess Angélique, and he was tired of answering the same question the same way every time one of those tin-plated jerks asked about her whereabouts.

"This lot doesn't look like they're from the High Kingdom," King Braxton said to the captain of his guards, who was standing next to him. "And unless I'm mistaken, King Rigderg of Cockaigne is with them."

The captain looked intently at the group making their way toward the castle. "I believe you're right," he confirmed.

"Then let's ride out and see what he wants with me and my realm," the King suggested.

King Rigderg signaled for everyone to halt. "King Braxton is approaching. Let me do the talking until we can meet with him in private."

Braxton, accompanied by thirty of his soldiers, rode out of the castle toward Rigderg and his traveling companions. Rigderg rode forward with his hand raised in greeting.

"Greetings, King Rigderg," Braxton said pleasantly. "Welcome to Arcadia. This is an unexpected pleasure. I hope this isn't a prelude to an invasion by your realm."

"Why would you think that, King Braxton?" Rigderg answered. "There are no grievances between our two realms that I'm aware of." Rigderg looked at Braxton curiously. "There *aren't* any grievances, are there?"

"None that I'm aware of," Braxton replied.

"Then there's no reason for me to invade your realm, is there?" Rigderg asked. "Besides, I've got enough problems without worrying about your realm."

The two kings grasped each other's right forearm in greeting. "It's good to see you again, my friend," Braxton said.

"I agree," Rigderg said. "If you're not too busy, my companions and I would like a word with you... in private."

"Private meetings between kings could raise suspicions," Braxton said with a wry smile. "With the High Kingdom's spies and soldiers running around, secrets are hard to keep these days. Suppose you tell me why you're here, and then I'll see if I have time to meet with you."

Rigderg nodded. "Fair enough. Where to start? First of

all, you remember me telling you about the questers who stopped Cockaigne's civil war, revealed that Viscount Ladrach had murdered King Diarmaid, and kidnapped my mother and Duke Berngal's wife and sister?"

"Of course."

Rigderg gestured toward his traveling companions. "Well, they surprised me yesterday with a visit. When I discovered they were heading here to speak with you, I agreed to come along and make introductions."

"You're here... to make... introductions?" Braxton looked at Rigderg with disbelief. "A fellow King? What aren't you telling me?"

"More than you can possibly imagine, my friend," Rigderg replied. "Shall we adjourn to your castle for that private discussion I mentioned?"

Braxton looked at Rigderg, then he looked back at Rigderg's traveling companions, and then back at Rigderg. "Oh, very well, since you're obviously not going to tell me anything now."

"It's not you, my friend, it's the number of ears that might be listening. These are perilous times, and I'm looking out for your neck, as well as my own."

Braxton nodded and led his unexpected guests back to the castle.

As they rode, Braxton asked, "What do you hear about the armies of the High Kingdom?"

"One is still where it was a couple of days ago," Rigderg answered vaguely. "But Telise's army is heading for Cockaigne sometime tomorrow."

"Do you need to be back there to greet them when they arrive?" Braxton asked.

Rigderg chuckled. "Not necessary. My mother will be

there to greet them, and when she's done with them, they'll wish they never stepped foot in Cockaigne or anywhere else on this continent."

"Why is that?"

"Because when Princess Telise's minion, Viscount Ladrach, kidnapped my mother and Duke Berngal's wife and sister, he made no secret that he was acting on Princess Telise's orders. Since the army about to descend on my realm is loyal to her, and my mother knows what kind of shenanigans Princess Telise is up to, Mother plans to give them a piece of her mind." Rigderg shuddered. "I've been on the receiving end of her rants, and I'm glad I'll be elsewhere instead of there. I don't want to be anywhere near her when she gets going."

Braxton laughed. "I've heard about women scorned, but a mother scorned? That must be gruesome indeed."

"You have no idea, my friend. No idea at all."

As they rode to King Braxton's castle, Nikki noticed a massive mountain range to the west of her. It was larger than any she had ever seen, and she wondered why she had never seen it from Cockaigne.

She pointed it out to King Rigderg.

"Ah, I see you haven't visited many of the realms," Rigderg said, smiling. "All of the realms are separated from each other by impassible mountains. That's why the portals were built in the first place. That mountain range runs right down the middle of the western continent, from the coast between Cockaigne and Arcadia, down to the coast between Riverstone and Asphodel. In fact, Riverstone and

Cockaigne share the only border in Annwyn that isn't marked by either a mountain range or the ocean. Of course, Riverstone isn't a realm, but it's vast, just as Cockaigne is."

"How vast?" Nikki asked.

"The Riverstone that most people see is mostly just the village and farmlands along the northern border. South of that, the territory spreads out for leagues, all the way to the sea along the west and south coasts. Supposedly, there are huge and ancient cities down there that are... abandoned. No one goes there, but I hear stories about them from time to time—mostly legends—but the cities are real. As for Cockaigne, the part that you've seen, bordered by the four castles, is south of the center of the realm. My lands extend far to the east, west, and north. This is probably why you never saw those mountains before. The hills around my castle hide them. If my population increases, there's plenty of land east and west where more villages can be built."

"What about the north?"

"Ah, well, there are wild forests north of the Viscount's old lands, and the northern coastline is all mountains. Plus, the northern coast is within sight of the island of Drakon, also known as the Island of the Dragons. They don't like the company of men, and men certainly don't like the company of dragons, so we keep people away from the northern coast. I understand there's a dragon colony in my coastal mountains, but I have no desire to find out for myself."

Nikki looked to the south. "So there's a mountain range the runs east to west separating Arcadia and Asphodel?"

Rigderg nodded. "You can't see it from here, but you

can from the top of King Braxton's castle."

"What about the eastern continent?" Nikki asked.

"The same," Rigderg answered. "There's a mountain range that runs from east to west that separates Elysium in the north from the rest of the realms. Then there's another range that runs east to west along the northern border of Avalona and the southern border of Brittia. A third range runs east to west across the northern border of Aaru and the southern border of Avalona. The mountains form a giant 'Z' across the continent."

"And the High Kingdom?" Nikki asked.

"It's the largest island on Annwyn," Rigderg answered, "so its borders are the ocean. Many still call the island 'Reingard,' which is the old name for that realm. There are many other islands, but only Reingard is inhabited, as far as we know."

They continued to King Braxton's castle in silence, and Nikki wished she could see a map of Annwyn again that showed the position of the mountains.

When they arrived at the castle, Rigderg's bodyguards and Princess Angélique's bodyguards were led to the barracks. The horses were taken to the stables. Braxton led Rigderg, the questers, and Princess Angélique—still disguised—to the great hall.

When they arrived in the hall, Braxton ordered everyone to leave and guards posted at the doors to see that they wouldn't be disturbed.

Once everyone had been seated, Rigderg introduced Livvy.

"My friend, this is Livvy-the-Sorceress. She's the one responsible for bringing down Viscount Ladrach's castle."

"I had help, your Majesty," Livvy said.

"A sorceress?" Braxton asked. "I thought you hated magical folk."

"I hate *wizards*," Rigderg corrected him. "Sorcerers are a different breed altogether. You know the new Grand Master is a sorcerer, and he's a good man. He helped Livvy destroy the late Viscount."

Braxton nodded. "And who are the rest of your companions?"

Rigderg introduced the rest of the questers.

Braxton noted that Rigderg didn't introduce Princess Angélique. "And who is the woman you didn't introduce?"

"She's the reason we're here," Rigderg said. "I had a fascinating conversation with her yesterday, and I found her to be a most extraordinary person. She's someone who listens more than she speaks, and she cares deeply about what's happening in the realms right now. She wants to have the same conversation with you that she had with me, and I cannot encourage you enough to speak with her. It'll be well worth your time."

Braxton snorted. "Laying it on thick, aren't you? Well, as long as she isn't from the High Kingdom. You know we had a troop of them pop out of the portal this morning and ask if we've seen the missing Princess? Like she'd ever be in this castle. Imagine!" Braxton looked at Angélique. "So? Who is she, and what's she here to talk about?"

Rigderg stood. "Your Majesty, she's here to talk about how we can avert a war and redefine how the realms will work together going forward. May I introduce to you Princess Angélique of the High Kingdom?"

Livvy transformed the Princess back to her true form.

Braxton stared at Angélique with his mouth open. His eyes bulged. He glared at Rigderg and then back at the Princess. Then he stood and reached for his sword, which was hanging on the back of his chair.

Angélique stood and held out her hands. "There's no need for that, your Majesty. I'm not my sister, nor am I my uncle. And I am just now beginning to understand how little I knew about how my family has been treating the realms. I want to do something about that, and I want to prevent the war that is getting ready to ravage Annwyn. I hope you will consent to attend a council of Kings to be held at the Grand Master's residence in Alesia, so we can all discuss what to do about my sister, the part of the army that's loyal to her, and the grievances held by the realms against the High Kingdom. But most of all, I want to prevent war, and I want to understand the realms better so I know how to work with each one to put an end to the conflicts that have been tearing us apart. I'm here to listen to you, your Majesty. I'm here to... apologize for what my armies did to cause the animosity you feel toward me."

Braxton stood frozen, his hand on the hilt of his sword.

"She's telling the truth, your Majesty," Rigderg said, moving next to the Princess. "I was skeptical, too, but she came to me in the company of these questers, to whom I owe... everything. I trust them with my life, and they trust her. Now I do, too. I wasn't sure before, but I am now." He looked at Braxton for a moment. "At least talk with her. There's no harm in that, is there? And then, if you don't believe her, or you don't want to meet with the other Kings to end all this nonsense, then let us go about our business, and we'll leave you alone to be about yours. There's no treachery here, old friend. Only an opportunity to make changes that won't come again."

Braxton's hand dropped to his side, and he sat down slowly. "And if what I have to say deals with how to abolish the High Kingdom and have your realm go back to being called Reingard again?"

"Then I want to hear that and your ideas of how the realms would interact with each other if that comes to pass," Angélique said sincerely.

Braxton stared at Rigderg and Angélique, and then he motioned for them to sit down. "I guess a conversation can't hurt, and if my old friend, King Rigderg, vouches for you, then I guess I can trust you." He cocked his head to the side. "I assume it goes without saying that this conversation never took place and you were never here?"

Angélique smiled. "It *would* be good of you to keep all of this a secret. If my sister finds out what I'm doing, I can assure you that nothing good will happen, and war will be the only option remaining. A war that no one can win."

Braxton and Princess Angélique spoke for hours. Rigderg interjected from time to time, but he mostly listened to the conversation. Livvy also interjected on occasion, but the questers didn't add much to the conversation.

Servants brought in lunch and supper, and Livvy transformed Angélique's appearance each time so no one outside the questers and the two Kings would see her in her true form.

Well after sundown, the conversation began to wane.

"Is there anything else you'd like to tell me or ask me?" Angélique asked Braxton.

The King shook his head. "I've said everything I've ever wanted to say to a member of your family, but never dared. Thank you for the opportunity."

"Are you willing to attend a council of Kings to discuss the present crisis and what we can do together to end it?" she asked.

Braxton thought about it for a minute. "Yes. I think a council of Kings is long overdue, and holding it at the Grand Master's house in Alesia will ensure the security of the attendees and what we discuss."

"Thank you, your Majesty," Angélique said.

"Will you accompany us to Asphodel to convince Tyrell to listen and talk to the Princess?" Rigderg asked.

Braxton snorted. "You're planning to talk to Tyrell next? You know he hates Telise and her late uncle. It won't be easy to keep him from killing the Princess out of spite."

"The Princess will be well-protected," Livvy said, "just like she was here, just like she was in Cockaigne."

Rigderg spun around and looked at Livvy. "You were protecting her all the time she was with me?"

"No, your Majesty, I was protecting her all the time we were in your castle. I'm doing the same now, and I'll do the same in every castle we visit."

Braxton laughed. "Now I see why people say it's best not to anger a sorcerer... or a sorceress. My compliments, Livvy."

"What about my bodyguards?" Angélique asked.

"What bodyguards?" Braxton asked.

"The troop who preceded us this morning," Rigderg said. "They're actually her bodyguards, not soldiers searching for her. They came through the portal before us to throw off any spies or traitors."

Braxton laughed again. "They did a very good job. I never suspected them. Why not send them through to Asphodel before we head there? It worked with me. It should work with Tyrell."

"Will they be safe in Asphodel?" Angélique asked.

"Relatively," Braxton replied. "As long as they're respectful and take 'no' for an answer, they shouldn't face any problems from Tyrell. He won't be happy to see them, but he will tell them what he knows in hopes that they'll leave quickly. By the way, where are these bodyguards?"

"Hiding in the woods behind the portal," Rigderg said. "It was my suggestion."

Braxton shook his head in disbelief. "And where are you going to have them hide in Asphodel? There aren't that many trees near Tyrell's castle."

"But there is the ruins of the old castle about three miles from the portal," Rigderg pointed out.

Braxton smiled. "That is an excellent suggestion."

Rigderg looked at Angélique. "Does that work for you, Princess?"

Angélique nodded. "Thank you for the suggestion, your Majesty. I'll have one of my guards here in the castle pass along that information at dawn tomorrow."

"And now I guess we should all get some rest," Braxton said, standing. "Tomorrow is going to be a busy day. I'll have my chamberlain show you to your quarters. They should be ready by now."

The questers were shown to their rooms, as was the Princess. Rigderg was housed in the royal wing closer to Braxton's bedchamber.

Nikki and Justin undressed, crawled into bed, snuggled close, and fell asleep almost immediately.

Livvy and Kevin did the same in their chamber. Livvy was exhausted, and Kevin could tell.

"Is there anything I can do to help you?" he asked.

"No, I'm able to handle what needs doing, but I don't think I can handle another resurrection anytime soon, so be sure to help protect everyone if we find ourselves under attack. Shield walls I can handle, and transformations, too. Just not cheating death of its prize."

"I promise," Kevin said.

Livvy snuggled close to Kevin and was soon asleep. Kevin just held her, but he stayed awake for much of the night, watching her and protecting her.

Allison crawled into bed as soon as she undressed. Peter joined her shortly after that.

"Why do you look at me differently?" Allison asked.

"I don't know what you mean."

"Yes, you do. Ever since I fell off my horse, you haven't looked at me the same way. Sometimes you look at me like you've never seen me before. Other times, you look at me like I'm going to vanish at any moment. I'm your wife, and I can't have you looking at me like a stranger or a broken doll. I need to know why, and I need it to stop."

"Allison, I'm not..."

"Not what, Peter? Not supposed to tell me something?

I have ears , you know. I know there's something Livvy told y'all not to tell me. But you're my husband, and we don't keep secrets from each other. Whatever it is, you *have* to tell me. 'Love, honor, and cherish,' remember? Well, you're not honoring our marriage, and you're not cherishing me if you're keeping secrets. Whatever it is, I can handle it."

"I'm not so sure," Peter said softly.

"And what's that supposed to mean," she demanded.

"It means that I don't know if you're ready to hear it. I don't know if you'll ever be ready to hear it. And if I'm right, and I do tell you, I don't want you blaming me for doing what you made me do."

Allison stared at him. "Is it that bad?"

Peter nodded.

"Well, it's not like I was dead or anything, so how bad can it be?"

Peter said nothing. He just stared at Allison.

"I wasn't dead, was I?" she asked slowly.

Peter still said nothing.

"I was dead?"

Peter nodded. "A crossbow bolt ricocheted off the back of Kevin's armor and hit you in the heart. You were gone before you hit the ground."

Allison reached for her chest, but she didn't feel anything. "Then how am I here?"

"Livvy and Bethany," Peter said. Then he explained how they healed her body and how Livvy brought her back.

Allison sat back and stared at Peter. "I remember that. Livvy said it was a dream, but I remember. I was surrounded by darkness. It was pitch black. My... body... was glowing, but the glow was fading, and I could feel myself slipping away. Then Livvy was next to me. She tried to lift me, but she couldn't. Then this incredible white light shone down on me, and I started glowing brighter. Livvy picked me up in her arms, and we started flying through the light, like it was a tunnel. The next thing I knew, I was on the ground with everyone standing around me, and Livvy looked like she had just run two marathons."

"You never mentioned that before."

"I thought I dreamed it," Allison insisted. "Livvy convinced me it was a dream caused when I hit my head."

"She never told us what it was like bringing you back," Peter said. "I think Kevin knows—he told me most of the story—but none of the rest do. All I know, besides what Kevin said, is that she brought you back, and it was the most exhausting thing she's ever done."

Allison shook her head. "So I was really dead."

"For several minutes," Peter said, "and they were the worst minutes of my life. I was in a fight against the guards that had just killed you, and I had to finish that. Then I ran back to see how you were, but Livvy and Bethany were busy repairing your body so Livvy could bring you back. I was falling apart at the thought of losing you, but Livvy had that firm, confident way of telling me that you were going to be all right, and I believed her. She made me believe she could do it. And she did. So if I'm looking at you differently, it's because I lost you, and then you came back. Part of me had already started grieving, and then, suddenly, there you were, and I was so grateful, but I was still grieving about losing you. Does that make sense?"

Allison shrugged. "I have no idea. I can't imagine what you went through. I didn't know a thing. I was on my horse, and then I was on the ground. What happened in between is blank, apart from my dream."

"Well, now you see why I didn't tell you any of this," Peter said. "The voice that communicated to Livvy told her that you wouldn't remember anything and not to tell you what happened."

Allison sat up. "What voice? You didn't mention a voice."

"According to what Kevin told me, there was a voice that told Livvy to summon the light, and then it told her not to let you find out about what happened."

Allison sat in silence for a while. Finally, she said, "Is that why you didn't want to make love to me last night? Are you afraid of me?"

Peter wrapped his arms around her. "No! I could never be afraid *of* you. I was afraid *for* you, like you might leave me again at any moment. I was afraid that being intimate might be too much and undo everything that Livvy did for you."

Allison took a deep breath and let it out slowly. "I never considered that. No wonder you've been looking at me weird."

"It isn't because I don't love you, it's because I can't stand the thought of losing you. And if I lost you because of something I did, it would kill me."

Allison held on to Peter. After several minutes, she suggested, "Well, what if I did all the work?"

"Meaning what?"

Allison reached beneath the sheets until her hand found what she was looking for. "What if you just lay back and let me do everything?"

"And what if the strain is too much?" Peter demanded, feeling her hand stroking him.

"Can you think of a better way to go?" Allison purred.

"Don't joke, Allison. I'm worried."

"So am I, but right now, I need to feel alive, and you're the best way I know to help me feel like that. We're going to have to do it at some point, if for no other reason than to make certain that we still can. The sooner we do it, the sooner we can get past all this and be ourselves around each other."

Peter was now fully erect, and he had to admit that there were no flaws in her logic. "Fine," he said, leaning back. "You do all the work the first time. If there are no problems, then we'll turn things up a bit. But if you get tired or woozy or anything like that, we stop, and I go find Livvy. Deal?"

Allison moved down so her head was next to his erection. "Deal," she said as she began licking his erection before putting it in her mouth.

Peter enjoyed the sensations, and soon he was lost in the passion—forgetting, for the moment, his concerns.

Allison continued letting her mouth do the work, and then she moved on top of him. She rubbed herself against his erection until she felt herself getting wet and sensitive. She lifted herself up and guided him inside of her. She moved up and down on him, and then she moved her hips forward and backward.

As Peter felt the sensations intensify, Allison increased speed until she felt him release. She was tired and breathing deeply, but she felt nothing out of the ordinary after what they had just shared.

"Willing to continue?" she whispered in his ear.

"Are you?"

Allison nodded.

Without breaking the connection, Peter flipped her

over so he was on top. He began thrusting, keeping their chests next to each other's so he could feel her heartbeat as they made love. Sensing nothing unusual, he raised up so he was on his knees. Allison arched her back so he could thrust deeply. He had one hand on her butt to hold her up, and he was stimulating her clit with the other hand. Allison climaxed, and Peter reached down and felt her heart. It was beating strongly, so he continued thrusting and stimulating her clit. She climaxed several more times before he rolled her over and penetrated her from behind.

Allison was on her hands and knees. Peter had one hand on her hip to hold her steady as he thrust. With the other hand, he reached around so he could stimulate her clit. She moved his hand out of the way to stimulate herself, and Peter used both hands to hold her hips.

Enjoying the sensations, Peter began thrusting faster and deeper. Allison climaxed several more times, causing her legs and arms to shake. At one point, she nearly went flat on the bed, but Peter held on to her. He felt his release building, and he increased speed.

A moment later, he came inside her, and she felt him release. She fell flat on the bed with him still inside her, and he lay on top of her, tired and satisfied.

They stayed like that for several minutes. Then Peter pulled out, and they cleaned each other off. Once that was done, Allison asked, "Does that convince you that I'm all right?"

Peter smiled. "If it doesn't, then nothing will. How do you feel?"

"Alive," Allison replied. "I feel alive."

They snuggled close and fell asleep.

# CHAPTER 10

The next morning, shortly before dawn, one of Princess Angélique's bodyguards rode to the woods where the rest of her bodyguards were waiting. He passed along her orders to travel through the portal to Asphodel, present themselves to King Tyrell, and then make camp in the ruins of the castle three miles from the portal.

Less than thirty minutes later, Braxton and Rigderg watched Angélique's soldiers disappear through the portal.

"You know we're committing high treason," Braxton said. "Just talking to Angélique is enough for us to lose our heads."

Rigderg watched the morning sunlight illuminate the mountain peaks to the west and the south. "And yet to do nothing will lead to the deaths of thousands of our people," he pointed out. "I'd rather risk treason for a chance at peace, than do nothing and be dragged into a war caused by Telise's mad ambitions."

Braxton nodded. "You're right. I just wanted to remind you of the risk we're taking."

"Noted. But if we're dead anyway, then let's die doing something, not because we did nothing."

Braxton slapped Rigderg on his shoulder. "Come, my friend. Let's eat before we tempt our fate in Asphodel."

The two Kings left the parapet and descended to the great hall, where the rest of their traveling companions were waiting.

The meeting with King Tyrell of Asphodel didn't go well at first. He had just gotten over the shock of his two neighboring Kings arriving unannounced, but the presence of Princess Angélique sent him into a rage. Tyrell was one of the kings who wanted to overthrow the High Kingdom by force, and the military preparations around his capital spoke of how soon he planned to invade Reingard and crush Princess Telise's few remaining forces.

Rigderg and Braxton tried to convince Tyrell to wait until the Kings could meet together, but in the end, it was Princess Angélique's willingness to listen and apologize for her family's past actions that caused Tyrell to agree to a delay in his invasion plans.

"Now that you've seen and heard what I'm planning, Princess, I'm not letting you out of my sight," Tyrell said, when he agreed to accompany the traveling companions to the four remaining realms. "If you decide to charge me with treason, your head will be mounted next to mine."

Angélique nodded. "Wanting to do something is not what I consider treason, King Tyrell," Angélique said.

"Acting on your plans is. As long as you don't invade the High Kingdom, then no crime has been committed. My sister may see things differently, but I don't."

"Then let's get the rest of the Kings together and talk about what we're going to do with your sister."

The Army of the High Kingdom loyal to Princess Telise caused problems for Angélique, the Kings, the questers, and the bodyguards when they reached the eastern continent.

When they arrived in Elysium, where Angélique's loyal soldiers had been hiding, they learned from the Portal Keeper that her army had been forced to redeploy to Cockaigne, because Telise's army was now in Elysium, searching for her and her soldiers.

The Portal Keeper kept them hidden until Telise's army redeployed to Asphodel. Angélique's loyal soldiers then returned to Elysium, and Angélique met with them before they returned to their previous hiding place. Then she, the Kings, the questers, and their bodyguards met with King Sebastian.

Unlike King Tyrell, King Sebastian was excited at the prospect of meeting with Angélique, and he quickly agreed to participate in a meeting with the other Kings to prevent the coming war. He and Angélique had been on friendly terms for years, which is why he was willing to hide her loyal soldiers within his realm.

King Wallace of Brittia, however, took much more convincing. He didn't like or trust the other Kings, he *hated* the High Kingdom, and he wanted to attack the other realms and bring them under *his* control, rather than under Angélique's or Telise's rule.

When Sebastian, Tyrell, Braxton, and Rigderg reminded him that, along with Angélique's loyal soldiers, he was outnumbered ten-to-one, he saw that his plans weren't practical, and he decided to listen. In the end, he agreed to meet with the other Kings to find a solution that was equitable for all.

Telise's army was in Avalona when Angélique arrived to meet with King Cullen. The Portal Keeper kept her, the Kings, the questers, and their bodyguards hidden until the army redeployed to Arcadia.

King Cullen, who was more like King Sebastian, was also enthusiastic to meet with Angélique and the other Kings.

King Carlton of Aaru wasn't. He flatly refused to speak with Angélique or the other Kings, and he refused to attend a meeting at the Grand Master's residence in Alesia. He wanted nothing to do with anyone. He just wanted to be left alone.

Seeing no alternative, Livvy intervened with King Carlton after everyone else had been shown to their quarters. She took control of his mind and convinced him to accompany them to Alesia. Once he was inside the Grand Master's residence, the control would be lifted.

The next morning, all seven Kings, Angélique, the questers, and the bodyguards approached the portal.

The Portal Keeper smiled and said, "Is everyone ready to travel to Alesia?"

Angélique replied, "Yes, please."

The Portal Keeper opened the Portal, and Thor, Bethany, Thor's assistants, and the other Portal Keepers—

including Ravana, the tavern owner—were waiting on the other side. The questers entered first, followed by Angélique and her bodyguards. Then the Kings and their bodyguards entered. The Portal Keeper was the last person to enter the portal, and the portal closed behind him.

The Spymaster of the High Kingdom, along with the army liaison with the royal council, entered the council chamber, where Princess Telise waited for them.

"What's so important that you had to meet with me this late at night?" Telise demanded.

"Your Highness," the spymaster began, "the army loyal to the High Kingdom has made some… strange reports that I thought you might want to know about."

"Define strange," Telise said irritably.

"Your Highness, as you know, the loyal army has been using the portals to travel between the realms, looking for your sister and her army," the Colonel said nervously. "Each time they enter a new realm, your commanders present themselves to the King of the realm before beginning their search."

"I know all of this," Telise stated.

"Yes, your Highness. But what's strange is this: for the last week, the Kings have refused to meet with your commanders. The underlings sent to receive your commanders give excuses why the Kings cannot meet, but the fact remains that your commanders haven't seen any of the kings for the past several days."

"And where are the Kings hiding?" Telise demanded.

"We have no idea," the spymaster admitted. "No one

has seen them. One moment they're in their castles, the next... they're gone. It could be that they're inspecting their soldiers or their lands, but all of them? At the same time? It seems a bit odd, and I thought you should know."

Telise drummed her fingers on the table. "Do you think they're planning something?"

"The High Kingdom *is* defenseless at the moment, your Highness," the Colonel said. "With both of our armies out in the realms, any one realm could conquer us with ease, assuming they could breach the gates of the city."

"And what do you suggest, Colonel?" Telise growled. "If we recall the loyal soldiers, my sister and her army could rally the realms and build a force large enough to conquer us. If I keep those soldiers out in the realms, looking for her and her army, she's pinned down and can't do anything."

"Yes, but the other realms still can," the spymaster pointed out. "And if they attack and destroy everything, then those two armies of ours won't have anything to return to. The High Kingdom will be left in ruins, and the realms will be free to do whatever they want. Our armies will have no authority to punish the realms, because there will be no one here to give those orders. With no pay, the armies will simply disband, and the High Kingdom, and the realm of Reingard, will fade into memory."

"Then what do we do? We're damned either way, so what's the least terrible solution to our problem?"

"I suggest we find the Kings first," the spymaster said. "Once we know what they've been up to, we'll know how to respond."

"Then work quickly," Telise said. "Find them, find what they've been doing, and report back to me. Now go!"

"Yes, your Highness."

The spymaster and the Colonel left the council chamber, uncertain about how to find the Kings or discover what they've been doing.

Angélique, the Kings, and the Portal Keepers met in the conference room of the Grand Master's residence, which none of the questers had seen before. Thor presided over the meeting.

The bodyguards were all camped outside the residence. The questers were given their usual guest chambers, and they opted to stay away from the council meeting until or if they were needed.

King Carlton was not happy to be there, but he promised that he wouldn't disrupt the proceedings. This was the first time that the Kings had been brought together to discuss their mutual problems. Normally, the High Kingdom would summon the Kings annually to inform them about new taxes or restrictions, but the Kings were never given the opportunity to discuss or debate anything. And the Portal Keepers were never involved in any discussions among the Kings. This had King Carlton curious enough to watch and listen.

After the introductions, Thor stood. "Let us be clear about one thing," he began. "A war that could kill thousands of innocent people is unthinkable, so any solution that leads to a general war between the High Kingdom and the realms is not an acceptable solution. The Portal Keepers are prepared to close all portals if you think that a war between the realms *is* a viable option. We are also prepared to close the Portal of Reingard in the High Kingdom if it looks like the Armies of the High Kingdom will be turned loose on the realms, and if they're already in the realms, then they will be trapped and unable to be deployed anywhere else.

"We need to identify how to end the current plots and intrigues of Princess Telise and the army units loyal to her. I don't care if the High Kingdom survives, or if the Eight Realms move forward without an 'overlord' telling them what they can and can't do. This council must decide the future of Annwyn—all of Annwyn."

Thor gestured toward Princess Angélique, and then he took his seat.

"Thank you, Grand Master, for hosting this meeting, and thank you all for attending," she began. "I agree with the Grand Master. After talking with each of the Kings, I also don't care if the High Kingdom survives. Frankly, my family has proven that it's not worthy to be anyone's overlords, as the Grand Master called it, and I know that most, if not all, of you agree with this. I am content for Reingard to be just another one of the realms, but if that is our decision, then we must determine how to bring that about with the least loss of life and property possible. Even though I'm a soldier, I have no interest in the future of Annwyn being paved in blood. There must be a better way to bring about the needed changes to our world, and I hope we can find that way before we all return to our realms."

Angélique sat, and everyone at the table applauded. King Carlton looked skeptical, but he clapped politely.

The Colonel, who was the army liaison with the royal council, walked into the spymaster's office.

"Have you heard the latest?"

The spymaster looked at the Colonel with disdain. "Can you be a bit more specific? I'm surrounded by reports from the realms about a hundred things."

"This is about the Portal Keepers," the Colonel said.

"What about them?"

"They're gone," the Colonel said. "None of the portals are currently in operation."

The spymaster looked at the Colonel. "Well, it's not unusual for the Grand Master to call meetings with all of his Portal Keepers. The new Grand Master has been doing it quite a bit lately."

"Yes, but those meetings rarely last longer than a day. This one has been going on for almost three days."

"Three? That *is* unusual," the spymaster confirmed. "That explains why I haven't had any new reports lately."

"And why the army can't move between the realms to look for Angélique and her army," the Colonel added.

"Hmmmm," the spymaster mused. "First the Kings, now the Portal Keepers. Is there a connection?"

"No idea," the Colonel said. "And now we have no way to find out."

"Did our Portal Keeper's assistants say when he'd be back or where he is?" the spymaster asked.

"They confirmed he's meeting with the Grand Master, but apart from that, they're being tight lipped. And after what happened to our previous Portal Keeper, I can't blame them."

The spymaster nodded. "Princess Telise won't be happy about this. If we can't use the portals to find the

Kings, she'll still blame us for not obeying her orders."

"Any suggestions?" the Colonel asked.

The spymaster shrugged. "I can't think of anything. Let's pray that the Portal Keepers return soon."

Allison found Livvy in the library with Nikki, and she motioned for Livvy to join her in the lounge across the hall.

When Livvy entered the lounge, Allison closed the door behind them so they wouldn't be disturbed.

"I know," Allison said.

"Know what?"

"What happened in Cockaigne at the portal," Allison replied.

Livvy blanched and then turned red. "How?"

"You people should really learn how to whisper," Allison said, sitting down and motioning for Livvy to sit. "I heard most of what you all were saying about what happened, and Peter provided the missing pieces. Plus, that dream I had wasn't a dream, was it? That was you trying to bring me back, right?"

Livvy sat silently.

"Look," Allison said, "I don't care if the voice told you not to tell me. I figured out most of it on my own, and now I know it all. I died that day, you and Bethany repaired my body, and then you brought my spirit back here and returned it to my body. Am I leaving anything out?"

Livvy shook her head. Then she asked, "Why did Peter tell you?"

"Because I made him," Allison said. "He's my husband, you know, and we made vows to each other. He had been looking at me so... strangely that I made him tell me why. I'm not sad that I insisted. I just needed to know."

"And now that you know you were dead and are alive again?"

"I don't know," Allison said. "I see the doctors I work with bring patients back to life all the time. We have babies that don't live more than a few minutes, and then the doctors bring them back, and they go on to have long and happy lives. How is this any different, except that I had a sorceress bring me back instead of a doctor?"

"No doctor could have brought you back from that wound," Livvy said.

"Then it's a good thing I had you, isn't it?"

Livvy smiled. "I guess it is. And for the record, I would have tried anything to bring you back. I'm just glad I was given the ability to do it."

"And now that you've done it, how do you look at life and death?"

Livvy took a deep breath and let it out slowly. "Honestly? I don't know. I still don't know if what I saw was real or just a representation that my mind could handle. But one thing I know for certain... wherever I was when I found you, I wasn't alone. Someone... something... was there with me, telling me what to do and guiding me back. I've never been particularly religious, but I have to think that God was helping me. I can't imagine any other being who would help me bring you back to life."

"So... we've both had a deeply moving religious experience, and we had to travel half-way across the universe to have it."

"I think you and I traveled a bit farther than that," Livvy pointed out. She looked at Allison. "Any after effects from what happened?"

Allison shook her head. "None. Peter and I made love in Arcadia… and Asphodel, and Brittia, and everything seemed normal. Peter was scared to death to try in Arcadia, but I forced the issue, and once we knew that I wasn't going to drop dead during sex, it became easier and normal again. I still don't know what to think about all this, and I don't think any of you are ever going to look at me the same way again—don't deny it. But I feel normal, and when we get back home, I'm sure this will become a distant memory, just like what happened to Nikki on the last quest is becoming a distant memory for her."

"I hope so," Livvy said. "You two are still my closest friends, apart from Kevin, and I plan on us being friends for a very long time to come."

"Me, too."

They both stood and hugged each other tightly. "Thank you for saving my life," Allison said.

"Always," Livvy responded.

The council meeting lasted for three days, and Thor had to step in and refocus the discussion several times when it strayed into unproductive topics and grievances.

By the end of the third day, the Kings and Princess Angélique had worked out how the Eight Realms would be structured, should their plans succeed. The High Kingdom would be abolished, and Angélique would rule the Realm of Reingard as an equal with the seven Kings. The rulers of each realm, along with the Grand Master—as a neutral party that controlled all transportation between the realms—would form a council of rulers that would deal with all matters affecting multiple realms, and the individual realms would be allowed to rule themselves on all matters that didn't affect other realms.

Since the Realm of Reingard was not in a position to be self-sustaining, thanks to centuries of dependence on taxing the other realms for food and income, it was agreed that the other realms would help Reingard become self-sustaining, since there was more than enough land for agriculture. The realm's gold mines, which were instrumental in helping it become the High Kingdom in the first place, would allow it to pay for the help it received from the other realms.

The more difficult agreement to reach was how to bring down Princess Telise and her army without an unacceptable loss of life. This required another day of discussions, and the questers were allowed to take part in crafting the strategy.

Because the Kings were not unified on how they wanted to "punish" the High Kingdom for centuries of tyranny, Nikki ended up presenting a strategy that the Kings and Angélique were willing to follow.

"Are your loyal soldiers still hiding in Elysium?" Nikki asked Angélique.

"Yes," Angélique replied. "They have to move from time to time to stay hidden, but with the Portal Keepers here, they have nothing to fear but Telise's spies finding them, and even then, the spies cannot report where they are until the Portal Keepers return to their realms."

"Can you show me on a map the terrain where they're hiding?" Nikki asked.

Angélique indicated where her army was hiding, and

King Sebastian supplied details on the terrain.

Nikki pointed to several of the natural features of the area that could give Angélique's army an advantage. Then Nikki sketched out how Angélique's army could be deployed. "If you deploy your army like this," Nikki said, "and allow Telise's army to know your location, then as soon as Telise's army arrives, they'd be flanked and forced to attack from a terrible field position."

"But what good would that do?" Angélique asked. "My soldiers wouldn't be able to counter attack easily, and any battle would be a stalemate."

"Exactly. That's what we want. Both armies together, unable to cause serious damage to the other."

"Why?" Angélique demanded.

"Because the combined armies of the realms will be invading and conquering the High Kingdom, while your and Telise's armies are distracted in Elysium," Nikki said.

"What?" Angélique wasn't sure she wanted the armies of the other realms turned loose on Reingard.

"Let me finish," Nikki asked. "The realms will send their armies to Reingard and conquer the High Kingdom. Once Telise and her cohorts are captured, and the High Kingdom has surrendered, then we redeploy the combined forces of the realms to Elysium, where they'll march on Telise's army from the rear. Her army will be surrounded by a vastly superior force and will have no choice but to surrender. Once they do, the war is over, and we can deal with Telise and her cohorts as necessary to prevent them from ever attempting to return to power."

"And then we draw up the treaties for everything we've agreed to so far," Thor added, "and once they're signed, everyone returns to his or her realm, and we begin a new age of peace and prosperity."

Angélique nodded slowly. "Where do you want me in all this? In Elysium with my soldiers, or with the combined armies of the realms invading the High Kingdom?"

"It might be best if you were with us invading your realm," King Braxton said. "Your people need to see you leading the combined forces. It might make them surrender faster, knowing that you're reclaiming what's rightfully yours. I can't imagine your people are too happy with Telise as their ruler."

"I doubt they are," Angélique confirmed. "Okay, I'll be part of the invasion of my realm, and then I'll lead the combined forces against Telise's army in Elysium."

Angélique looked at King Sebastian. "Your Majesty, are you okay with the final battle taking place in your realm? If you'd prefer, we can move the battle to another realm. The overall strategy will still work."

Sebastian smiled. He looked at the map for a moment, and then he said, "This is a fairly unpopulated area of my realm. There should be no civilians inconvenienced by the strategy, and these natural formations will be necessary for the plan to work. Keep the plan as is. I like the idea of the last battle on our world taking place in my realm."

Angélique bowed to Sebastian. "Thank you, your Majesty."

"Is there anything else we need to discuss?" Thor asked.

"Just some details," Nikki said. "Princess Angélique, how many soldiers are still in the High Kingdom?"

"Between two hundred and three hundred," she replied.

"And how good are the fortifications around the palace

and the capital city?"

"Quite good," Angélique admitted. "It cannot be taken by siege, the walls are too thick to be damaged by any weapons we have, and the foundations are too firm to knock down or pull down the outer walls. The only vulnerability is the gates, and once they're closed, the outer defenses will make the gates very difficult to breach. A small force can hold the city against a very large force for quite some time."

"Time we don't have, if we're to get to Elysium before the High Kingdom's armies tear each other apart," Nikki noted. She looked at Livvy. "Looks like we're going to need some specialized assistance breaching the walls so the combined armies can take the city before anyone inside can get organized to resist."

"Are you thinking dragon fire, or do you want me to just obliterate the foundations so the walls collapse?" Livvy asked.

"You can do that?" King Wallace of Brittia asked.

Livvy nodded. "We destroyed Viscount Ladrach's castle that way several months ago."

"Which way is the easiest for you?" Nikki asked.

"Probably dragon fire," Livvy replied. "Blasting foundations will take a lot of effort. Transforming a few of you into dragons will be much easier... and impressive. You'll be able to direct your fire just at the walls and gates, sparing the civilians from injury. If I blast the foundations, rock will be blown in all directions, and that's what we're trying to avoid."

"How many dragons do we need?" Nikki asked.

"How large are the outer walls?" Livvy asked.

Angélique shook her head. "They're huge."

"Can you form a picture of the walls in your mind and let me see it?" Livvy asked.

Angélique nodded. Livvy looked into Angélique's mind and saw the High Kingdom's capital city.

"Wow," Livvy said. "I had no idea it was so large or so beautiful. I imagine you want to preserve what's inside the walls?"

"If possible," Angélique said. "But do what you have to do so the city surrenders to the combined forces of the realms."

Livvy sat back and thought about what she had seen in Angélique's mind. Then she said, "We'll need four dragons for this."

Kevin and Nikki stepped forward, as did Justin and Peter.

"Justin, you and Peter are new to being dragons. You'll need to practice like Nikki did before we deploy with Princess Angélique to the High Kingdom."

Justin and Peter nodded in agreement.

"You actually have the ability to transform your companions into dragons?" King Carlton asked.

"Yes," Livvy replied.

"Then why do you need my army?" he demanded.

"Because dragons incinerate people, and we're trying to spare lives. If we wanted everyone dead, we wouldn't need your or anyone else's army. But we're trying to keep people alive and end this conflict peacefully. Your army is needed to convince the High Kingdom that it cannot win against the combined forces of the realms. The dragons are just there to knock down their defenses. We're trying to redefine how the realms will interact when this is all over, and you don't do that by murdering innocent civilians, no matter what grievances you have against them."

Ling Carlton slammed his hands on the table loudly. "I want vengeance against the High Kingdom," he cried. "I want my pound of flesh. They've been murdering my people for centuries. I want them to have a taste of what that feels like."

Livvy looked at Thor, who stood up. "It is clear to me that Aaru's King has very different ideas on how to resolve this conflict than the rest of us do. I'm afraid I have no choice but to close Aaru's portal once King Carlton has been returned to his realm. This is for the good of the rest of the realms."

King Carlton stood and glared at Thor. Thor stared back, saying nothing. He didn't flinch, he didn't blink, and he didn't back down.

The full weight of Thor's words began to sink in, and Carlton's hands began to tremble. "You'd really isolate my realm from the rest of Annwyn?"

"To prevent loss of life? Absolutely," Thor confirmed.

"For how long?"

"For the rest of your life," Thor said. "And if your successors share your bloodlust, then the portal will remain closed until your bloodline fades into obscurity."

Carlton looked around the room, and he saw that he had no allies at the table. He slowly sat down. After taking a moment to compose himself, he said, "Very well. If everyone agrees to the plan, my realm will comply, and for the good of my people, I'll forgo any acts of vengeance against the High Kingdom from this moment on."

Thor sat and nodded. Then he recapped the plan that Nikki and Livvy had presented. When he was done, he called for a vote, and it passed unanimously.

"Is there anything else we need to discuss while we're all together?" Thor asked.

"One thing," Angélique said. "The forces from the realms will have to come through their portals to reach the High Kingdom, which is on the hill overlooking the capital city. That makes our staging area visible to the city's defenders. We'd have to arrive at night and deploy around the city immediately. That means that each realm would have to send its army through at precisely the same time. Should we bring all of the armies from the realms to a single place outside the High Kingdom, and then send them all through a single portal so they can arrive outside the city at the same time?"

"That is a very good suggestion," Thor said. "How long will it take each realm to gather its forces, and does anyone have a staging area sufficient for this campaign?"

"Elysium is out of the question," King Sebastian said. "Both of the High Kingdom's armies will be engaging when we invade Reingard. That's too much chaos for my realm to handle."

Thor nodded in agreement.

King Rigderg stood. "Cockaigne might work. There is a massive open space between my castle and the river that could hold our combined forces. It will take a week or two to gather my army. Once that's done, you can begin bringing your armies through the portal so we're all ready to invade Reingard together."

The other kings agreed that they'd need at least a week if not two weeks to gather their armies and reach the staging area.

"Then we'll meet in Cockaigne in two weeks," Angélique said. "We have that long to trap Telise's army in

Elysium and begin our invasion. Is everyone in agreement?"

All of the kings nodded, as did the Portal Keepers.

"Then I think we have everything covered for now," Thor said. "If there are no objections, I declare this council meeting concluded."

Everyone in the room applauded.

Thor motioned for the Portal Keepers to follow him to the corner of the room. "I'll send each of you back to your portals first. No doubt Telise's spies have noticed that you've all been gone for at least four days. They'll have intelligence that they'll want to get to the High Kingdom, including reports of your absence. Feel free to send them to the wrong realms for the next week or two so they can't report anything until the kings are home and gathering their forces. As for Telise's army, they must not be allowed in Cockaigne or the High Kingdom under any circumstances, and they cannot be allowed into Elysium until we're ready to invade the High Kingdom. We'll use the portals and our assistants to coordinate our actions."

The Portal Keepers smiled and nodded.

Thor asked the Kings to stay for lunch while he sent the Portal Keepers back to their portals. Thor's assistants brought in food, while Thor and the Portal Keepers left the residence.

The questers stood together in the opposite corner of the room. "Is anyone as nervous as I am?" Nikki asked.

"Absolutely," Livvy said. "This is going to be huge, with a lot of moving parts, and it could all fall apart quickly if we're not all careful."

"What am I going to do during the attack on the city and Telise's army?" Allison asked.

Bethany, who had been standing with the questers, replied, "You're staying here with me. If they need healers, we'll go through the portal to help, but if not, we'll stay here until it's all over."

Allison started to protest, but Bethany whispered, "Besides, I have questions that require your particular expertise."

"What expertise are you referring to?"

"Obstetrics," Bethany answered softly.

Allison's hand flew up to her mouth. "You mean you're—"

"Shhhh," Bethany hissed. "Not so loud. I'm not sure. That's why I want you here to help me figure it out. I don't have access to the tools and resources I had on Earth, so I need an expert in the field to guide me."

Allison beamed. "Okay. I'll help you, but if the others need us, we go, okay?"

Bethany nodded.

# CHAPTER 11

The Kings and their bodyguards left for their realms shortly after lunch to start gathering their armies, leaving Angélique, her bodyguards, and the questers in Alesia with the Grand Master and Bethany.

"How do you feel the council meeting went, Princess?" Thor asked as they walked back to the residence.

"I'm encouraged by what we accomplished," she replied, "nervous about what we're about to attempt, both with the High Kingdom and afterwards, and I'm a bit worried. Can you really change the world peacefully without bloodshed?"

"It hasn't happened often," Thor remarked. "But empires forged in blood never last, as we're seeing now with the High Kingdom. All it takes is a single spark to bring the empire to its knees, and Telise accusing you of murder was that spark. When you create a government of equals, where interactions are based on mutual respect and value, rather than edicts and tyranny, you stand a better chance of a long and lasting peace. And if there's an effective way to address grievances going forward, then there are fewer opportunities for that peace to be broken. But it takes work, Princess. Complacency is the enemy of peace. Evil thrives in complacency, and that can destroy a realm—or the world—faster than any spark, because it eats from within everything good you've built. Once it begins to corrupt and defile, it's very hard to eradicate and repair the damage, because eradication and repairs require action, and complacency creates an environment of inaction. That's when tyranny begins to flourish again, starting the cycle that we're trying to break by what we're doing. If you keep that in mind and are vigilant, you can avoid the mistakes that all too many governments in the past have made. Never forget that."

"I won't, Grand Master," Angélique said. "I swear."

"On a different topic, Princess," Thor said as they approached the residence, "there's no need for you to travel to Elysium today. I've given instructions to the Portal Keepers that Telise's forces are not to be allowed to travel there until we're ready to spring the trap. I offer the hospitality of my home until you're ready to leave."

"Thank you, Grand Master. I feel at peace here. And I want to say again that I'm very sorry my sister tried to wrestle control of your portal from your predecessor, and that she tried to kidnap your betrothed in an attempt to blackmail you into surrendering your portal to her. Even though she's my sister, I utterly condemn her actions."

"Thank you, Princess," Thor said, "but it's unnecessary. You took no part in her schemes."

Angélique nodded. "It still pains me just how far she was willing to go to break the rules that have defined our world since the ancient beings visited here eons ago. The independence of the portals is key to the balance of forces keeping Annwyn together. It should never have happened, and I'll do all I can to see that it never happens again."

Thor smiled. "I appreciate that, Princess."

When they reached the residence, Angélique followed Thor to his study. "Do you mind if I ask you another question?" she asked.

Thor gestured for her to sit in one of the wingback chairs by the fireplace. He sat in the one opposite her. "Be my guest."

"By tradition, no Portal Keeper or Grand Master has ever gotten involved in the political aspects of Annwyn before, as far as I know. But you're the true architect of the largest political change this world has seen since the High Kingdom came into existence. Why?"

Thor smiled. "If your sister's henchmen hadn't kidnapped my predecessor and my betrothed, if it hadn't been her plan to seize control of the portals and the realms so she'd be the sole ruler and power on Annwyn, it's entirely possible that I would have let things continue on as they have for countless centuries. But tradition or not, I could not and will not stand idly by and watch this world go up in flames for the evil of one person or one family—not when I have the means at my disposal to stop it. I wasn't kidding when I said that I'd shut down whatever portals necessary to preserve life and stop your sister's plans. If the realms cannot work together, and if the High Kingdom can't govern wisely and honestly, then those with the means to resist are duty-bound to do so. I have at my fingertips the means to force the realms to do whatever I want them to do, but if I did that, wouldn't I be simply a replacement for what I'm resisting? No, I won't use the portal to make myself absolute ruler. But I will use them to preserve life, and if that means that the High Kingdom is brought down, then so be it. Power corrupts, and your family has become the embodiment of that. I won't follow your family down that hole, but I will use the tools at my disposal to prevent your family from destroying the realms for its own selfish ambitions. Your sister has to go, but it has to be by the consent of all of the Kings, not on the orders of one man who happens to be Grand Master."

"So you turn your back on absolute power, even when you hold it in your hands?" Angélique asked, astonished.

Thor nodded. "I have a job... one that has been handed down faithfully since the ancient beings first visited us. I'm not here to rule or to force my will on others. I'm here to advise and keep the portals functioning for the benefit of the realms and Annwyn as a whole. I may have advised the Kings regarding a plan of my making, but they're the ones who had to approve of that plan, and they're the ones who will execute it. I'll help, but change must come from this world's leaders, not from me. I shared my ideas, but if the Kings had chosen a different path, I'd do my best to support it, provided it wouldn't lead to war, bloodshed, or the eventual destruction of the realms."

Angélique shook her head. "All my life, I've been surrounded by people struggling for power over others. And here you sit with more real power than any man on this world, and yet you limit it to serve, rather than to govern or control. I didn't know such things were possible."

"Oh, I may impose limits on myself so I don't overstep the boundaries of my position," Thor said, "but I'm also a resident of this world, and as such, I'll take action to prevent harm to others where I can. I may seem different from my predecessors, but I possess all of their memories, so I know what they would've done if they faced what we're facing. I believe they would've acted, too. The difference is, as a historian, I see repeating patterns over the eons, what worked and what failed, and I have different ideas about how to act. That's all. But in the end, I'm still just the Grand Master, and the protection of the portals is my responsibility. When your sister became a threat to that responsibility, then the removal of that threat became my responsibility, too. Once she has been dealt with, then I can go back to performing my primary duties and leave politics to the realms."

Angélique sat back and thought about what Thor had said to her. She tried to understand, but it was difficult. Thor was not like anyone she had ever met, and that frightened her. But she trusted him.

"May I ask one more question?"

Thor smiled. "Of course."

"Where are we?"

"In Alesia," he answered with a smile.

"Yes, but where is Alesia?"

"On Annwyn."

Angélique frowned. "Can you be more specific?"

"Let me put it this way," Thor replied. "We're not on the Island of the Dragons, we're not on the Island of Reingard, and we're not on the eastern or the western continent. But there's more to Annwyn than those four places, and Alesia is one of them."

"But you're not going to tell me exactly where it is?"

Thor shook his head. "By *tradition*, no one can know. Your sister found out, and look at what happened. If that isn't proof of why this place must remain secret, then I don't know what is."

Angélique nodded. "And if I find Telise's map showing the location of Alesia when all this is over?"

"Then I'd appreciate you burning it and forgetting what you saw," Thor replied.

The captain of King Rigderg's guards met the King at the portal when he returned from Alesia.

"Welcome back, your Majesty," the captain said. "Were your travels successful?"

"More than I ever imagined they'd be," Rigderg replied. "Why were you waiting for me here?"

"When the Portal Keeper arrived a few hours ago, I thought you might be returning soon. I wanted to speak with you... in private."

Rigderg looked back at his bodyguards. "Return to your barracks and begin carrying out my instructions." Looking at his captain, he pointed toward the river. "Shall we ride and talk that way?"

The captain nodded, and the two rode west.

"What's going on?" Rigderg asked.

"Spies from the High Kingdom have been looking for you, your Majesty," the captain answered. "And the army of the High Kingdom was not happy that your mother met with them instead of you."

Rigderg chuckled. "I can just imagine."

The captain laughed. "It was quite a performance your mother gave. I've never seen fear in the eyes of soldiers from the High Kingdom before, but I swear the commanding officer soiled himself... twice."

Rigderg laughed.

"You laugh, Sire, but they'll report back to the High Kingdom, now that the portals are working again, and it could go very badly for Cockaigne. Their spies all went through the portal about thirty minutes ago."

"And they're hopelessly lost in the other realms by now," Rigderg said, "as is Telise's army. No one is going to report anything to the High Kingdom until the right moment."

"I don't understand," the captain said.

Rigderg pulled his horse to a stop and explained what happened at Alesia, the plans that had been made, and the visitors that would be arriving in the next week.

"We're really going to invade the High Kingdom and abolish its rule... forever?" the captain said, shocked.

Rigderg nodded. "Every realm will bring their armies here, and then we march on the High Kingdom together. Once the capital city surrenders and Telise is captured, Princess Angélique will be named the Queen of the Realm of Reingard. There will be no more High Kingdom. Annwyn will be ruled by a council, consisting of the rulers of each realm and the Grand Master. Together, we will decide what needs to be done for the benefit of all realms, not just one."

The captain nodded. "What do we need to do now?"

"It's being done, Captain. A party is riding to Duke Berngal's castle to have him bring his army here, and my bodyguards are riding across this region to call up all able-bodied soldiers. I want our army assembled before the other armies begin arriving."

"And put them where?" the captain asked.

Rigderg gestured toward the empty fields around them. "Here. This is the staging area for the invasion. The Kings will be housed in the castle, and the soldiers will fill these fields. It'll be the first time that the armies of all the realms will be in one place at the same time."

"Aren't you worried that fights might break out?"

Rigderg smiled. "No. The four dragons that'll be part of the invasion force will be preparing themselves here, too, and if there's any fighting, the dragons will take care of it for us."

"Dragons, your Majesty?"

Rigderg nodded. "Four of them. We'll need them to breach the walls of the High Kingdom's capital city. We'll also need them to convince Telise's soldiers to surrender."

The captain had a look of confusion and awe on his face. "How did you get dragons to agree to fight alongside humans?"

"Oh, I didn't. Livvy-the-Sorceress did. She'll be here in the next couple of days to oversee the dragon training."

The captain shuddered. "And who will lead the invasion?"

"Princess Angélique has the overall command of the combined armies of the realms," Rigderg replied.

They turned their horses and rode back to the castle.

"Is there anything else I should know?" the captain asked.

"Probably," Rigderg replied, "but there will be plenty of time to discuss that once our guests start arriving."

"Yes, your Majesty."

Angélique went to bed early that night. She, the questers, and her bodyguards were leaving for Elysium in the morning to meet with her army, and then they were traveling to Cockaigne to wait for the other armies to arrive at the staging area.

Thor, Bethany, and the questers sat in the study, talking about old times and how their lives had changed. Livvy, knowing that she needed to conserve her strength for what was to come, left the others and went to bed.

"How is she?" Thor asked, concerned.

"She's been through a lot," Kevin answered. "Between protecting Angélique 24-7, changing her appearance several times a day, transforming some of us into dragons, not to mention what happened in Cockaigne, it's a wonder she's still standing."

"She's the most powerful sorceress this world has ever seen," Thor said. "The portal at Riverstone saw to that. But she still has limits. Keep a close watch on her once the invasion begins. She needs to conserve her strength."

"I will," Kevin promised. Then he followed Livvy to their chamber.

Nikki and Justin were the next to leave, leaving Allison and Peter with Thor and Bethany.

"How are you feeling?" Thor asked Allison.

"I'm fine, Thor," Allison assured him. "No ill effects at all."

Thor shook his head. "I remember when the tavern owner first talked to us about resurrections, but I never really thought he was serious... or that it was possible."

"It's possible, all right, but the tavern owner left out quite a bit information that would have been good for Livvy to know," Bethany said.

Thor nodded. Then he said to Allison, "Well, I'm happy you're still with us, and I agree that it's best that you stay here unless you're needed during the invasion. Livvy is going to be under tremendous strain, and there are limits on what I can do to help. The fewer civilians she has to worry about, the better."

Allison nodded. "I wish I were going to be there, if only to see Peter as a dragon."

"You've seen dragons before," Peter said.

"Yes, but not you as a dragon."

Peter nodded.

They talked for a while longer, and then Peter and Allison went upstairs to their chamber.

"It's remarkable," Thor said to Bethany as they left the study together.

"What is?" she asked.

"That Allison is still with us. What Livvy did is the hardest magical thing that can be done, and she did it by herself. If you hadn't been there to show her what an undamaged heart looks like, she could never have done it. So many things had to happen in just the right way for Allison to be alive right now. If that doesn't make you believe in a higher power, I don't know what will."

Thor and Bethany put their arms around each other as they walked to their chamber.

As soon as Nikki and Justin reached their chamber, it became clear that Nikki didn't want sleep just yet. Once the door was closed and locked, Nikki took charge.

"Take your clothes off," she said.

Justin complied in record time. Nikki watched him, admiring his body in the firelight.

"Pull over that chair." She pointed to a chair next to the fireplace. Justin grabbed it and pulled it closer to the bed.

"Now remove my clothes."

Justin quickly removed Nikki's clothes and set them next to his own.

Nikki walked over to the basin of water on the night table, wet one of the towels, and returned to stand in front of Justin. She washed him, spending a little extra time on the part of him that was already getting stiff. Then she ordered Justin to wash her.

Justin took another towel, wet it, and washed Nikki thoroughly, rubbing the cloth gently across her breasts, her butt, and between her legs. Nikki was already quite wet, but she enjoyed Justin's attention to her sensitive spots.

When he was done, Nikki pointed to the chair. Justin sat, and Nikki straddled him, allowing his erection to penetrate her immediately. With both hands on the back of the chair, she began to raise and lower herself on his lap, moaning as his erection went deep inside of her.

Justin's hands were free to roam, and he massaged her breasts before reaching behind and clutching her butt. Nikki increased speed. Her muscular body moved rapidly, and her skin glistened in the firelight. Justin tried to hold back, but his release couldn't be denied. He came deep inside of her.

Nikki didn't stop. She continued moving up and down on him.

She did this for several minutes, until Justin released a second time inside of her. Nikki stopped moving and sat on him, kissing him and running her fingers through his hair.

She reached over for a clean towel, stood, and wiped herself off. Then she wiped Justin off. She tossed the towel on the bed and walked around to the other side. She stood in the far corner and beckoned Justin to come to her.

He didn't have to be encouraged twice.

Nikki stood with her back to the corner. Justin pressed against her, grabbed her wrists, and lifted her arms above her head as he kissed her. He was fully erect again, and he wanted to be inside of her. He released her hands, and she put her arms around his neck.

Justin grabbed her butt, and Nikki wrapped her legs around his waist. She moved one hand down to guide him inside, and then she clung to his neck as he began thrusting, pressing her against the wall to keep her in place.

Nikki's arms tightened around his neck as she pressed herself against him as closely as she could. Their sweat provided lubrication as she slid up and down against him from his thrusts, stimulating her breasts and causing her to climax again and again.

Just as the next climax subsided, Justin pulled out, turned her around, and pushed her toward the window. The curtains were not entirely closed, and Nikki was standing in front of the opening. Justin forced her to lean over, with both hands pressed against the glass. Justin massaged her butt and then penetrated her from behind, holding her hips as she steadied herself against the window.

The firelight illuminated her leg and butt muscles, and her skin glistened with sweat from the fire's heat outside and her hot core inside. Her wetness frothed and ran down her inner leg as Justin thrust deeply and rapidly. Then he pressed his chest against her back, reached around, and began stimulating her clit, causing her to climax several more times.

Justin released inside of her again.

Nikki still hadn't had enough.

She grabbed the towel from the bed, wiped herself and Justin off, and lay on the bed.

"Make me squirt," she purred.

"Are you sure?" Justin inquired.

Nikki nodded.

Justin grabbed a few more towels, spread them on the side of the bed where Nikki was lying, and got on the bed next to her. Then he began to stimulate her clit and her pussy, bringing her orgasm after orgasm until she finally sprayed the towels on the bed, squealing loudly.

"Again," she moaned.

He obliged, and she squirted a second time, spraying more and farther than the first time. Her squeals intensified in volume and duration.

Then he moved on top of her and penetrated her, thrusting as he continued massaging her clit rapidly. She squirted again, and Justin pulled out before penetrating her again and thrusting more rapidly. His hand moved back and forth across her clit, lubricated by her wetness.

Nikki felt the strongest orgasm ever about to hit, and when she felt Justin release inside of her again, her body lost all control. Her arms flailed, as did her legs, and she bounced on the bed—squealing louder than before—her stomach muscles and hip muscles clenching and contorting as the orgasm tried to shake her apart.

Panting and out of breath, Justin pulled out, grabbed

the rest of the clean towels, and began to wipe off the mess from between Nikki's legs. Then he washed her again all over to remove the sweat.

After he had washed himself, he piled the dirty towels in the far corner of the room and joined Nikki on the bed.

"Are you all right?" he whispered as she snuggled close to him.

"I think I'll recover," Nikki replied, exhausted but feeling wonderful.

"What was that all about?" he asked.

Nikki rubbed his chest muscles. "We're leaving here tomorrow, we have two battles to fight... as dragons, and we have a world to change. If we don't make it back home, I wanted one night with you worth dying for."

"And did you get what you wanted?"

Nikki nodded. "More. I got more. You?"

"It was amazing, that's for sure," he said. "Having you take charge like that was interesting, but I liked it."

"You didn't mind?"

"No."

"Good," Nikki said, "because I have one last present for you to show my appreciation for what you did to me tonight."

"I'm not sure I have anything left to give," Justin said.

"Then let me do the giving," she purred as she moved down and began letting her tongue stimulate him.

He wanted to tell her to stop, but he couldn't. It felt too good, and he knew she wanted to do this.

He let her.

Between the tightness of her lips and the way her tongue darted around, stimulating the head and shaft, the sensations were mind-blowing. He stroked her hair as she took everything left inside of him. He began trembling uncontrollably, but she didn't stop. His legs began shaking, but she didn't stop. His hands pulled her hair back, but she didn't stop.

And when he finally released in her mouth, she giggled with delight as the hot liquid shot down her throat.

Justin lay there, unable to move. Nikki grabbed the one remaining clean towel, wiped him off, wiped off her mouth, and tossed the towel across the room onto the pile of dirty towels on the floor.

"I can't believe I came again," he said. "Thank you for that, but no more. Not tonight. I can't."

"I can't believe I had the strength left to do that," Nikki said. "I'm completely spent right now. If one of Telise's soldiers burst through the door, I'd tell him to run me through, because I'd never be able to lift my sword."

"Me either," Justin said.

Without bothering to cover themselves, they moved closer to each other and fell asleep.

# CHAPTER 12

The next morning, Justin heard a light tapping on the door. He rose, feeling stiff and tired, and crossed the room to see who was there. He cracked the door open, but he saw no one. Looking down, he noticed that someone had left a fresh basin of water and several more towels. He fought the urge to laugh, grabbed the basin and towels, and closed the door.

When he returned to bed, Nikki stirred. "Did you get up just now?"

"Yes," Justin whispered. "Sorry I woke you."

"Why?"

"Someone knocked on the door. They brought us more water and fresh towels."

Nikki chuckled. "I guess we made some noise last night."

"We? I think you mean *you* made some noise last night."

"Fine. I made some noise, and you made a mess. If you

didn't cum so much, we wouldn't need so many towels."

"I regret nothing," Justin said softly.

"Neither do I," Nikki agreed. "About you cumming or me screaming."

"And squirting," Justine reminded her. "Don't forget that."

"How could I. I still can't figure it out, but I love it."

They lay next to each other for a while. Then Nikki sighed. "Well, I'm awake now."

"I can't," Justin said quickly.

Nikki playfully swatted him on his shoulder. "Not that, silly. I mean I might as well get up and get dressed. I'm hungry."

"So am I," Justin said. "Let's wash, dress, and go downstairs."

They crawled off the bed, grabbed the fresh towels and water, and began to wash.

Even in the low light of the fireplace embers, Nikki's body was radiant, and if Justin had an ounce of strength left in his loins, he knew he'd be fully erect from the sight of her. But after the night before, there was no way he was going to have another erection anytime soon.

Once bathed, they dressed and crept downstairs. The smell of fresh bread baking told them that Thor's assistants were up. Nikki blushed slightly, but hunger won over her modesty, and they entered the kitchen to see what was for breakfast.

Nikki and Justin had just finished eating a fresh-baked loaf of bread when Livvy and Kevin entered the kitchen. Livvy took one look at Nikki and started giggling. Nikki blushed furiously, but what could she say? Livvy had clearly heard everything that happened in Nikki's room the night before.

Livvy and Kevin sat across the table from Nikki and Justin, and a few minutes later, Allison and Peter entered the kitchen. She, too, giggled when she saw Nikki.

"Did everyone sleep well?" Allison asked innocently.

"Except for the banshee wailing down the hall," Livvy said.

Everyone at the table, and two of Thor's assistants, burst out laughing.

Nikki covered her face with her hands, but she was laughing, too.

"What are you all laughing about?" Angélique asked when she entered the kitchen.

"Nikki's impressive vocalizations last night," Allison responded.

Angélique grinned and looked at Nikki. "So that's what I heard. I was starting to believe the residence was haunted."

Everyone started laughing again, and Nikki put her head down on the table, covered by her arms. Justin patted her back, but he couldn't stop laughing.

Bethany and Thor entered the kitchen. Bethany took one look at Nikki, and she knew what the others were laughing about. "Perhaps we should discuss the plans for today and give poor Nikki a break," Bethany suggested. "It's clear she didn't get much sleep last night, and her vocal cords are probably in need of some rest."

Angélique nearly fell out of her chair, she was laughing so hard.

Thor tried to keep a straight face, but it was difficult

for him, and soon, tears were streaming down his face. "All I can say is thank you for waiting until the Kings had left for their realms. I wouldn't have wanted them too frightened to ever return here in the future."

Nikki looked defiantly at her friends. "I'm not the only one who has been a bit noisy since we started this quest," Nikki pointed out. "I seem to recall Livvy and Allison contributing to the ghost stories of some of the castles we visited."

"Yes, but I doubt they had the volume or the echoing quality of your voice," Thor stated quietly. "I was afraid the villagers would complain that their sleep was being disturbed last night."

"At least I had something to scream about," Nikki muttered as Thor's assistants served breakfast to everyone. She glanced at Justin, who was looking very proud of himself, and she grinned at him.

"Please," Kevin said. "I'm trying to eat here."

After breakfast, Angélique went out to check on her bodyguards, who were camped behind the residence. Thor's assistants had been keeping them well fed, as well as taking care of their horses.

"We're heading to Elysium to give the army its final orders before the invasion of the High Kingdom," she said to the captain of her guards. "How long will it take you to break camp and be ready to leave?"

The captain of the guards was surprised that Angélique was asking this question. She usually barked orders, and he and his men did their best to obey.

Consulting with soldiers was something out of character for a Commanding General.

"Thirty minutes, General," the captain replied.

Angélique nodded. "I think it will take our traveling companions slightly longer. Have the men ready to go in an hour."

"Yes, General."

Angélique entered the Grand Master's residence and informed the others that she'd be leaving for Elysium in an hour—undisguised. She needed to be seen by her sister's spies as part of the overall plan.

"Will you go straight to Cockaigne from there, or do you plan to come back here first?" Thor asked.

"Straight to Cockaigne," Angélique responded. "I want to be there as the realms bring their armies to the staging area." She turned to Livvy and added, "I'd also like to watch the dragons practicing for the assault against my city. I should be able to provide some suggestions on where they should attack first."

"Good plan," Thor said.

An hour later, when Angélique and the questers stepped outside the residence, Angélique's bodyguards were already mounted, and Thor's assistants had everyone else's horses saddled and ready to go—everyone except Allison, who was remaining behind with Bethany.

Allison and Bethany said their goodbyes to the questers, and then Thor mounted his horse and led the questers, Angélique, and her bodyguards to the portal.

When they reached the portal, everyone dismounted and prepared to lead their horses through. Thor opened the portal, and Elysium appeared on the other side.

"Good luck, my friends," Thor said to the questers.

Then he turned to Angélique. "Good luck, Princess. I have every confidence that you'll usher in a golden age for Annwyn by what you're doing."

"Thank you, Grand Master. I hope to see you when this is all over."

The questers entered the portal first, followed by Angélique and her bodyguards. Thor waved to them one last time and closed the portal. Then he mounted his horse and rode back to the residence.

"How far away is your army?" Justin asked.

"About five miles that way," Angélique said, pointing northwest. "There's an inlet there, and the army is deployed in a clearing tucked into a large rock formation that keeps it out of sight."

Angélique turned to the Portal Keeper, who had just arrived to see who had come through the portal. When he saw Angélique, he smiled.

"Good Morning, Princess," he greeted her pleasantly.

"Good Morning," she responded. "We'll be heading to Cockaigne in a few hours. Will you be here to open the portal for us?"

"I shall be here all day, Princess," the Portal Keeper assured her, "and I'll send word to you in Cockaigne once Telise's army arrives here next week."

Angélique nodded. Then she mounted her horse, and she, her bodyguards, and the questers rode for the inlet where her army was hiding.

Finding the army was not a problem, and when she was recognized, her soldiers began cheering. She ordered them to gather around her so she could share her news.

She told them about the meeting in Alesia, the plan for her soldiers to trick Telise's army into engaging them, and the realms' invasion of the High Kingdom to capture Telise and the capital city. She then told her soldiers that the armies of the realms would join them to force Telise's army to surrender.

"It has become clear to me that the High Kingdom, and particularly my family, has become toxic to the Eight Realms," she explained. "The other realms never wanted to be controlled by a single authority, and they look at us as tyrants, rather than peacekeepers. It is time to abolish the High Kingdom and return to being the Realm of Reingard. That is what will happen once my sister has been captured, our capital city has surrendered to the combined forces of the other realms, and the other half of our armies has been defeated in this place by you and the armies of the other realms. Believe me when I say that this is what's best for Annwyn, even if it may not seem to be what's best for us. I ask you to trust me."

Most of her soldiers didn't fully understand the plan, but they trusted Angélique, and they were happy that the conflict would soon be over and they could return home.

Angélique spent the next two hours with her Generals and Colonels, mapping out where the soldiers should be deployed when Telise's army arrived. The natural rock formations in the area would protect her soldiers and be almost impossible for Telise's army to scale or flank without suffering severe losses.

Satisfied that her officers understood their orders, Angélique wished her soldiers good luck against Telise's army, and then she, her bodyguards, and the questers headed back to the portal.

When they reached the portal, the Portal Keeper was smiling. "You were seen, Princess. Several of the High Kingdom's spies saw you arrive, and they know where your army is hiding. They tried to get back to the High Kingdom with this news, but I'm afraid they ended up in Brittia instead. I doubt that King Wallace will be happy to see them, so there's no telling which realm they be sent to next, once the Portal Keeper in Brittia allows them to travel again. I understand his portal is in need of maintenance. It could be several days before anyone can leave that realm."

Angélique laughed and thanked the Portal Keeper.

Angélique, her bodyguards, and the questers arrived in Cockaigne in the darkness of early morning. Even though they had left Alesia mid-morning, and had left Elysium late that afternoon, Cockaigne was on the opposite side of Annwyn, where the sun had yet to rise in the east.

The Portal Keeper greeted them, having been warned by the Portal Keeper in Elysium that they'd be arriving that morning.

"How go the preparations?" Angélique asked the Portal Keeper.

"They're well underway," the Portal Keeper replied. "None of the other forces are here yet, but King Rigderg's forces have started gathering. Speaking of the King, I informed him that you'd arrive this morning. He's waiting for you at the castle."

She thanked the Portal Keeper, and then she and the questers, followed by her bodyguards, rode for the castle.

The King, his mother, and the captain of his guard were waiting at the top of the causeway leading to the castle's main gates.

"Good Morning, Princess," Rigderg said pleasantly. "Welcome back. Your chambers are being prepared, and food is cooking as we speak. If you'll dismount, my grooms will see to your horses."

Angélique dismounted. "Thank you, your Majesty. Preparations have begun in Elysium. Now we wait for the armies of the realms to arrive."

Angélique's bodyguards were escorted to the barracks, and the King led the Princess and the questers to the great hall, where the smell of fresh-baked breads and roasting meats filled the air.

After a hearty breakfast, Angélique and the questers rode out to the north edge of the fields where the realms' armies would be staged for the invasion of the High Kingdom. Livvy wanted Nikki and Kevin to help Peter and Justin learn how to be dragons, so they'd be ready for their part of the invasion plan.

Nikki and Kevin, who had been dragons before, had no difficulty learning to fly or attack while in the form of the great four-footed beasts. But for some reason, neither Peter nor Justin could get used to the weight distribution of having four legs *and* wings.

After trying a number of dragon breeds, Livvy decided to transform Justin and Peter into wyverns, which are a type of dragon having only two legs and small claws at the tip of each wing—like bats—to help it grip rocks and timbers when on the ground.

Justin and Peter found this shape easier to handle, and while wyverns tended to be smaller than standard dragons, they were faster and more ferocious in battle.

Angélique watched in fascination as the four questers flew and performed a variety of aerial acrobatics while they learned to work in unison for the attack.

"I never realized there were so many different kinds of dragons," Angélique said to Livvy as they watched the dragons practice flying.

"Each one has different strengths," Livvy noted as she watched Peter spin toward the ground, only to pull up at the last second and soar away. "Nikki and Kevin are the more traditional dragons, and their four legs are excellent at knocking down towers and breaking apart walls. Peter and Justin, though, are wyverns, and their two legs aren't as useful at breaking apart fortifications. They're still quite capable of knocking over towers, but their real power is in their fire. They can unleash fire with such force that towers will collapse with ease, and they fly so fast that they can be gone, leaving destruction in their wake, before any surviving defenders can shoot back at them."

"How would you deploy them?" Angélique asked.

"To take out guard towers and upper wall defenses, I'd send in the wyverns first. They'd shred the upper walls in a short time. Then I'd have the dragons knock down the walls, leaving the city defenseless. The wyverns would also be good at bursting open the gates. While the dragons destroy the walls, I'd have the wyverns fly through the city, striking terror into the hearts of the occupants. And if it becomes necessary to damage the city to force its surrender, the wyverns would be better suited for that kind of work."

Livvy looked at Angélique. "I know you don't want to damage the city, but we have to prepare for all options to achieve the victory we need."

Angélique nodded, watching Justin and Nikki fly around each other. "They're lovers even as dragons," she marveled.

"Yes, but the two breeds are incompatible, so they can't act on it."

Angélique stared at Livvy, and then she laughed.

The dragons practiced attacking the capital city for the next week. There were several rock formations along the northern edge of the fields, and Livvy had the four dragons use them as the guard towers and city walls. By the end of the week, there was little left of the rock formations, apart from gravel and scorched earth.

Nine days after Angélique arrived in Cockaigne, Duke Berngal and his half of Cockaigne's army rode into the staging area.

King Carlton of Aaru came through the portal with his army that afternoon. Rigderg greeted Carlton and showed him where his army would be camped. Then he led Carlton to the castle so he could settle into his quarters.

King Tyrell of Asphodel and his army came through the portal the next morning, followed by King Cullen and the army of Avalona that afternoon.

King Braxton from Arcadia arrived the morning after, followed by King Wallace of Brittia two hours later. That afternoon, King Sebastian of Elysium brought his army through the portal.

All of the realms' armies were now gathered at the staging area for the invasion. All that remained was to receive notice that Telise's army and the High Kingdom's spies were all trapped in Elysium.

Livvy had the questers continue their dragon training—not as much because they needed more training, but because the armies needed to be accustomed to the dragons being around.

Angélique and the Kings met each day to review the plans, and they worked with the combined armies to ensure that the soldiers deployed quickly once they were through the portal. Angélique explained the terrain around the capital city of the High Kingdom, so they'd know what to expect when they arrived.

The armies were as ready as they could be.

"Grand Master, the armies of the realms have gathered in Cockaigne."

Thor nodded at the news Milos had just brought him. Milos was one of his assistants, and he was one of the two assistants on duty at the portal to receive news from the Portal Keepers. "Then tomorrow we let the High Kingdom's spies all be sent to Elysium, and the day after that, we send Telise's army there."

"I'll make certain those instructions are passed to all Portal Keepers," Milos offered.

Thor nodded, and the two men walked down the hill from the residence so Thor could open the Portal and Milos could deliver the messages across Annwyn. The eve of battle had arrived.

The High Kingdom's spies arrived in Elysium, and they became enraged when they saw that they weren't in the High Kingdom.

The Portal Keeper came out to greet them. "You're back! I guess you've heard that Princess Angélique's army is here in Elysium."

The spies looked dumbfounded. "They're here? We haven't heard. Where are they?"

The Portal Keeper gave them directions to Angélique's army. "I'll inform Princess Telise's soldiers that they're here. You can show them the way when they arrive."

The spies raced off to find Angélique's soldiers. The Portal Keeper and his assistants returned to their quarters, laughing as quietly as they could.

At dawn the next morning, Telise's army began arriving in Elysium from Asphodel, where they had been stranded for over a week. It took hours before the entire army had arrived, since the Portal Keeper in Asphodel only allowed the soldiers to enter one at a time. It was getting dark in the cold evening before the army was ready to start marching on their foes.

The spies, who were waiting for the army to arrive, described the location of Angélique's army and the defensive position they had selected.

"I'd advise waiting until just before sunrise before attacking," the ranking spy said. "If you march in there now, you'll never be able to see them, but they'll be able to see you. The outcome of that engagement could be terrible."

The Commanding General of Telise's forces nodded. "We'll make camp here for the night, and then redeploy before dawn."

The Portal Keeper, who had been listening to the conversation between the spies and the General, sent a message to Cockaigne, letting the Portal Keeper there know that the combined armies of the realms could begin their invasion at any time.

When Angélique received word that the armies of the High Kingdom were trapped in Elysium, she informed the Kings.

"The time has come, and we can begin the invasion of Reingard in three hours. It'll be dark there by then, and we can deploy under the cover of night."

The Kings went to inform their armies and remind the men that the goal was to get the city to surrender and to capture Princess Telise. There would be no looting or massacres of the residents of the High Kingdom. The invasion was to be as bloodless as possible.

Livvy and the questers stayed close to Angélique. Cockaigne's army, which had been given the honor of the first position in gratitude for their hospitality, would enter the portal first. Angélique, her bodyguards, and the questers would go next, and the other armies would follow. The men would enter the portal in columns of six across to speed up the time it would take to get all of the armies from Cockaigne to Reingard.

Livvy planned to keep a shield wall around Angélique at all times. Livvy also intended to transform her fellow questers into dragons as soon as they arrived in Reingard, which would give her time to recover from the effort before the battle began.

When the Portal Keeper opened the portal to Reingard, the soldiers could see the lights of the High Kingdom's capital city beyond. King Rigderg, with Duke Berngal at his side, entered the portal, followed by his army. Angélique, the questers, and her bodyguards followed. Then the rest of the realms' armies entered the portal for the invasion to liberate the realms and Annwyn forever from the tyranny and corruption of the High Kingdom and Angélique's family.

The soldiers of the realms' armies deployed quickly as soon as they came through the portal. Even though it was night, the torches around the capital city gave the soldiers enough light to see where they were going.

Angélique rode to her position for the invasion. She, her bodyguards, and Livvy would be in the middle of the causeway leading to the city's main gates—just out of bowshot. The Kings would join her once their armies were in position.

Livvy looked at her companions. "Are you ready for this?" she asked.

They nodded and dismounted, handing the reins of their horses to four of Angélique's bodyguards. Then they walked in front of Livvy and waited.

Livvy concentrated, and Nikki and Kevin were transformed into dragons, while Justin and Peter were transformed into wyverns. They moved around to the rear of the armies, waiting for the signal that would begin their attack on the city.

Princess Telise was awakened the next morning by the sound of someone banging on her door. She looked at the man in bed next to her, and she realized she didn't even know his name.

Hearing the pounding on her chamber door continue, she rose, put on her robe and stormed across the room to see who was disturbing her.

"What is it?" she demanded as she opened the doors.

The spymaster and the Colonel, serving as the army liaison to her council, stood in front of her, looking panicked. "Your Highness," the spymaster began, "we've been invaded!"

"By whom?" Telise growled.

"The realms, your Highness."

"Which realms," she demanded.

"All of them," the Colonel answered. "The combined armies of all seven realms have surrounded the city, and the Kings are on the causeway, demanding that the city surrender and that you be arrested."

Telise snorted, knowing the strength of the city's defenses. "Anything else?"

"Princess Angélique is with them, your Highness," the spymaster said. "She's leading the armies against us."

"Where are our armies?" Telise shrieked.

"We have reports that both armies are engaged in Elysium," the Colonel responded.

"Recall them at once!" Telise demanded.

"We can't, your Highness. The Portal Keeper says that the Grand Master is preventing travel to and from Elysium."

Telise was enraged at the news. She pushed past them and ran to her balcony. As she leaned on the stone railing, she looked out at the tens of thousands of soldiers surrounding her beautiful city. She saw Angélique in her armor, and she saw the seven Kings on their horses right behind her sister.

Looking behind her sister and the Kings, she saw something that made her heart freeze. Sitting on the ground were four huge beasts that she had only read about in books. “Are those... are those...?”

“Yes, your Highness,” the Colonel confirmed. “Those are dragons, fighting against us alongside Angélique’s forces.”

# CHAPTER 13

Telise stared at the scene in front of her. "Where the hell did she get dragons? There haven't been any seen in the realms in eons."

"There are rumors that there's a dragon colony on the north coast of Cockaigne, just south of the Island of the Dragons, but these are unconfirmed. But wherever they came from, they're here now, and they appear to be ready to attack the city."

"With no army, all we have are the three hundred soldiers in the city garrison. How are they to stand against thousands of soldiers from the realms," she demanded. "How long can they hold the city walls?"

"Against the soldiers?" the Colonel answered. "Weeks... months... even years, as long as we have food and no one dams the river. Against dragons? Maybe ten minutes."

"What?" Telise screamed.

"Dragons are the most destructive beasts ever

created," the Colonel said. "If your sister unleashes them against us, we'll be lucky to survive until noon. They'll raze the city to ruins and kill everyone before we can notify our armies about what's happening here."

Telise stared at her sister. "What do I do?" she whispered.

"Ask for terms of surrender," the Colonel replied. "This is a fight we can't win."

Telise turned on the Colonel. "You know they'll want me arrested, along with all of my advisors, don't you?"

The Colonel and the spymaster both nodded.

"And you're willing to be exiled... or executed... with me?"

The two men nodded again. "To save the city? Yes," the Colonel stated.

Telise looked around again. Then she said, "I'm getting dressed. When I come back, you two had better have another plan."

Angélique watched as the city garrison took its positions in the guard towers and on the outer wall. Then she saw her sister appear on the turret to the left of the main gates.

"What are you doing here, murderer?" Telise taunted.

"I'm here to arrest you for murdering our uncle, and for the crimes you've committed against the realms and against the Grand Master. I'm here to dissolve the High Kingdom, returning these lands to their former position as the Realm of Reingard, and I'm here to reclaim my throne, which you attempted to steal from me through your treason. You have ten minutes to comply."

"Or what?" Telise shouted. "You don't have enough men to breach these walls, and once our armies return from Elysium, you won't have enough soldiers to demand anything of me."

"Have your eyes deceived you?" Angélique asked. "Or do you not recognize that I have four dragons with me, who will reduce those walls to rubble in minutes?"

"You wouldn't dare."

Angélique raised her arm, and the four dragons took to the air, roaring and sending shivers of fear down the backs of everyone who heard the terrible sound. Justin flew directly at the main gates and shot fire from his mouth. The gates were obliterated, as was part of the right turret. Justin banked and flew back to the others.

Telise ordered the city garrison to protect the gates.

Angélique watched this, shaking her head. "Do you actually believe that those brave men can stop the forces under my command? Surrender now, and I'll spare the city. Refuse, and I'll unleash everything I have on you until you agree to my terms."

"I will never surrender to that rabble from the realms, or to your giant lizards. This is the High Kingdom, and it will remain the High Kingdom, even if I'm the only one still alive when this is all over."

"So be it," Angélique said. She turned and nodded to the dragons.

Telise never imagined that so much destruction could be caused so quickly.

Justin and Peter, working on opposite sides of the

gates, began their attacks. The upper walls and guard towers were demolished in minutes, sending brick, stone, and plaster to the ground on both sides of the walls.

While Justin and Peter attacked the turrets on either side of the gates, Nikki and Kevin began attacking the walls themselves, blasting huge holes in them from the inside out and using their legs to kick over chunks of stone onto the ground.

Telise and her men abandoned the walls and retreated into the city, while the four dragons ripped the outer walls apart like they were made of paper.

"Your Highness, we must surrender," the Colonel implored. "You can't let the city be demolished simply because you're afraid to face the consequences of your actions."

"How dare you talk to me like that?" Telise screamed. "That's treason!"

"No, your Highness, letting your people be killed for *you* is treason," the colonel said, drawing his sword.

"Don't you threaten me, Colonel. I still rule here."

"Your sister rules here now, your Highness. You're under arrest." The colonel placed the tip of his sword against Telise's throat. "Don't make me kill you."

The spymaster ran up to the Colonel. "The armies of the realms have entered the walls and are storming the city!" he said. Then he looked at the Colonel and Telise, and he noticed the Colonel's sword for the first time.

"What are you doing?" he demanded.

"Arresting this traitor before the entire city is destroyed," the Colonel answered.

The spymaster looked at the Colonel, then Telise, and then back to the Colonel.

"Help me!" Telise shouted to her spymaster.

The spymaster drew his dagger. But Telise's smile of triumph quickly faded when the spymaster turned the dagger on her.

"Bind her hands, and let's tell her sister that we surrender," the Colonel ordered.

"Right," the spymaster agreed. He yanked the cords holding back two nearby curtain panels and used them to bind Telise's hands. The Colonel tied a white cloth to his sword blade. Then, with the spymaster on one side and the Colonel on the other—holding his sword blade high so the white cloth could be seen—they led Telise outside to find Angélique and end her assault on the city.

It took nearly ten minutes to find Angélique, who was still near the main gates with the Kings. As the Colonel and the spymaster approached, Telise began thrashing. Fortunately, the spymaster had tied the cords too tight for her to escape.

"Here is the prisoner you requested, your Majesty," the Colonel said as he approached Angélique. "The city surrenders to your forces."

"Thank you, Colonel," Angélique said. "You and the other members of my sister's council are also under arrest until we can sort out who conspired with her and who merely accepted her false accusations at face value."

Both the Colonel and the spymaster bowed, accepting their fate.

Angélique looked at Livvy. "Recall your dragons. Their job is over."

Livvy nodded and reached out to the dragons with her mind. *"We have Telise in custody. Break off your attack."*

Nikki, Justin, Kevin, and Peter flew to an open field

outside the city and landed.

Seeing the dragons up close as they flew overhead, Telise fainted.

Angélique turned to King Rigderg. "Your Majesty, will you and your army hold the city for me until I return. Two of the dragons will remain here to make certain that the city isn't molested and that the residents don't try to counter attack once we've left for Elysium."

"It will be my honor, Princess," Rigderg replied, motioning to his bodyguards to seize Telise, the Colonel, and the spymaster. "Is there anyone else who needs to be arrested?"

"Yes. Every member of the King's Council. I need to discover who is guilty and who is innocent among them. I also need to make certain that the treasury is secured so no one tries to loot it."

"I'll see to it," Rigderg promised.

Angélique turned to the other Kings. "Rally your men, your Majesties. It's time to redeploy to Elysium and end this once and for all."

It took two hours to withdraw the soldiers from the city and begin the march up to the portal.

Livvy asked Kevin and Peter to remain in Reingard to support Rigderg's men holding the city. Looting or sabotage by the city residents was to be dealt with harshly, and no one was to attempt to escape from the city before Angélique returned. Kevin and Peter agreed, and they rose into the air to begin patrolling the skies around the city.

Turning to Nikki and Justin, Livvy said, "I need the

two of you to come with me to Elysium, in case you're needed to help convince Telise's army to surrender."

*"We're too big to go through the portal,"* Nikki said.

"I'll shrink you when we go through the portal, and then I'll return you to your normal size on the other side."

Nikki and Justin agreed. Livvy shrunk them, and they perched on her shoulders for the ride to the portal.

It took another four hours for the realm's armies to reach Elysium.

Nikki and Justin were returned to their normal size as soon as Livvy came through the portal, and they flew ahead to see what the two armies were doing.

"Nikki and Justin have reached your armies," Livvy said to Angélique a few minutes after the dragons flew off. "Your soldiers are in the rocks, and Telise's soldiers are in the clearing. Neither has a clear shot at the other, and neither can attack the other safely. It's a stalemate."

"Perfect," Angélique said. Looking to the Kings next to her, she said, "Let's proceed with the next phase of the plan."

It was early afternoon in Elysium when the combined armies began marching to the inlet where the two armies were skirmishing. Telise's army was so busy trying to dislodge Angélique's soldiers from the rocks that no one noticed the soldiers moving into the clearing behind them.

The High Kingdom's spies did.

They alerted Telise's Commanding General, who turned around and realized that he was caught in a trap. And when he saw Angélique leading the combined forces, he was furious that he hadn't anticipated this when the Portal Keepers kept sending him to the wrong realms.

He ordered his soldiers to form a second line of battle to the rear. He was determined to die for the High Kingdom, not knowing that the High Kingdom had already surrendered to Angélique's forces.

Livvy saw Telise's soldiers redeploying, and even she could tell that there was going to be a costly fight unless something was done to prevent it. She told Nikki and Justin, who were hidden behind a large rock formation, to convince Telise's forces to surrender.

*"What do we do?"* Justin asked Nikki.

*"First, we destroy all their wagons. That'll eliminate their supplies. If that doesn't work, we take out the leaders, who are probably in the center. After that, we use fire to keep the armies from attacking each other."*

*"I'll follow your lead,"* Justin said.

When Nikki and Justin appeared, rising from their hiding place, Telise's soldiers cried out in terror.

*"Watch for arrows,"* Nikki said as she flew toward the supply wagons.

Justin flew faster, and soon the supply wagons were reduced to smoldering ash.

Nikki saw a company of archers getting ready to fire, and as much as she didn't want to kill them, she couldn't have them shooting at her or Justin. She released her fire, and the entire company was incinerated in seconds.

"Surrender, General," Angélique shouted, "or your army will be destroyed. The High Kingdom has already surrendered to the combined army of the realms, and my sister has been captured."

Angélique gestured toward the dragons, flying

overhead. "This is a battle you cannot win. Surrender, and you will be spared."

The Commanding General didn't respond.

"Any soldier who lays down his arms and steps forward will be spared," Angélique shouted.

Almost two-thirds of Telise's army threw down their swords, shields, bows, quivers, and pikes. Then they threw down their daggers and walked toward Angélique and her armies from the realms.

"Get back in line or be executed for desertion!" the Commanding General shouted at his men.

The men didn't listen.

"You can't execute them for deserting an army I've already ordered disbanded," Angélique shouted to the Commanding General. "The Realm of Reingard doesn't need an army large enough to keep the other realms in line. The High Kingdom no longer exists. We only need enough soldiers to protect our own. The rest are free to become farmers, ranchers, merchants, tradesmen, and anything else we need to be self-sufficient as a realm equal with the others. This is your last chance to surrender. If you don't, your life is forfeit."

"Do your worst!" the Commanding General shouted. "Long live High Queen Telise!"

Angélique glanced at Livvy who nodded.

*"End this,"* Livvy said to Nikki and Justin.

Once the deserting soldiers had reached the safety of the realm's armies, Nikki and Justin dove towards the remaining soldiers loyal to Telise. Fire flew from their mouths, incinerating men by the hundreds with each pass. The Commanding General was killed in the first pass, as were all of the senior officers who hadn't deserted. Archers tried to bring the dragons down, but Angélique's archers in the rocks fired their arrows, taking out Telise's archers before the dragons could be injured.

After several minutes, none of Telise's loyal soldiers and spies, or the weapons laid down by the deserting soldiers, remained—only ash, smoke, twisted metal, and the stench of dragon fire and burning flesh.

A great cheer rose from the combined armies of the realms, which was answered by a cheer from Angélique's soldiers in the rocks. The fighting was over. The High Kingdom was over. The war was over.

"What happens now, Princess?" King Carlton of Aaru asked as Angélique's army left the rocks and formed ranks alongside the combined armies of the realms.

"We did what we set out to do, your Majesty," she replied. "I think it's safe to send our armies home. I'd like the Kings and their retainers to come back to Reingard with me. I need to be crowned Queen of Reingard, and then we collect the prisoners and return to Alesia together. I understand the Grand Master wants to meet with us and the Portal Keepers to sign the treaties formalizing what we decided the last time we were there. After that, the prisoners will learn their fate."

"Dragon snacks?" Carlton asked excitedly.

"I don't know what the Grand Master has in mind," Angélique admitted. "His grievances against my sister are as lengthy as mine, so it'll be interesting to see how we can accommodate both of our needs to extract punishment."

King Sebastian smiled. "I've certainly enjoyed having

the final battle of the High Kingdom take place here in my realm. My army has already been released, so I'm free to accompany you to Reingard and then Alesia."

The other Kings agreed to send their armies home and accompany Angélique to Reingard and Alesia.

Since each army was heading for different realms, it took longer to send them home than it did to bring them to Reingard and Elysium. It was a day and a half before all of the armies were safely back in their own realms. All that remained were the former armies of the High Kingdom, the Kings, Angélique, Livvy, and Nikki and Justin, who were back in their human forms.

Angélique used the time to meet with her officers. "We need to determine how large of a standing army Reingard needs, and how to choose which soldiers will stay and which ones will be released from duty to pursue other trades," she said to them.

"Can we agree that the soldiers who fought for Telise, but deserted rather than be destroyed by the dragons, will be released from duty immediately?" the Commanding General of Angélique's army asked.

"Yes," Angélique confirmed. "I'd rather not have them in the army, but they've earned the right to live in peace."

After hours of debate on how large the army of Reingard should be, Angélique suggested that it shouldn't be the largest nor the smallest army of any of the realms. She had the numbers for each army that participated in the invasion of Reingard, and after settling on the average number of soldiers from the other armies, the officers realized that Reingard would only need a third of the current soldiers loyal to Angélique to remain in the army.

"That's two thirds of your loyal army that will be released from duty upon our return to Reingard," the Commanding General noted.

Angélique nodded. "And now we need to select who will remain in the army and who will be released from duty. We need the right mix of mounted troops, foot soldiers, and archers, as well as auxiliary troops, such as blacksmiths, healers, cooks, scouts, messengers, supply staff, and such. How do we make those choices?"

"I think it might be best to choose by units, rather than individuals," the Commanding General suggested. "For example, if we have ten units of archers, but we only need three, then we keep the three best and release the other seven. We do the same for foot soldiers and mounted soldiers."

Angélique looked at the other officers. "Do you all agree with this method?"

They all nodded.

"Excellent suggestion, General. Let's get to it."

The officers determined the number of mounted units, foot soldier units, and archer units that would be needed, plus auxiliary units. Then they identified the best units in each category. Selecting the soldiers to retain with the army became a much easier task at that point, and the decisions were completed before the last of the realms' soldiers had left Elysium through the portal.

"We'll notify all of the soldiers when we return to Reingard," Angélique decided. "Let them return home in triumph before we release them."

Her officers agreed.

By the time Angélique returned to Reingard, the soldiers from Cockaigne had restored order to the city, captured the rest of Telise's advisors, and discovered several caches of embezzled gold, stolen from the High Kingdom's treasury by the finance minister and other advisors. Angélique pledged some of the recovered gold as severance to the soldiers being released from duty.

Peter and Kevin were returned to their human forms. They were famished by this point, and food was brought to them quickly.

Angélique met with her people to explain what was happening and what abolishing the High Kingdom meant for the realm. Her words were met with a mixture of reactions.

"I knew they wouldn't be thrilled," she said to Livvy as they watched the sunset in the distance, "but I hoped they'd understand why this has to happen."

"Change isn't easy," Livvy said. "It takes people time to understand what the change will do to *them* before they can decide if it's a good thing or not. Give them time, but don't wait for them to agree before making the changes that have to be made. Show them progress, show them how they fit into their new world, show them the opportunities that change can create. The rest is up to them."

The army of Cockaigne was sent home that afternoon, as the new Army of the Realm of Reingard was able to maintain order with no difficulty.

The next morning, Angélique was crowned Queen of the Realm of Reingard. The original crowns from before the High Kingdom came into existence had been melted down centuries earlier, and Angélique didn't want to wear the High Kingdom's crown. Goldsmiths worked tirelessly to create a new crown, fitting the ruler of a single realm. It had two wings on either side, rising from a gold circlet.

Angélique thought about being crowned in her military uniform, which was like a second skin to her, but now that she was no longer the Supreme Commander of the Armies of the High Kingdom, she felt she needed to be crowned as a civilian.

It was the first time that her subjects had seen her as anything other than a soldier. The dress she wore was russet-colored, which set off her auburn hair beautifully. She was stunningly beautiful as a woman, something that no one had ever seemed to notice before.

There was a banquet after the ceremony, attended by the Kings, the questers, and some of the more prominent citizens of the city.

After the banquet, Angélique appointed and met with her new ministers to make certain that they understood their roles and how she expected them to perform their duties. She also ordered the crowns of the High Kingdom to be melted down, and the gold returned to the treasury. All of Telise's possessions were to be sold off, and the money returned to the treasury. The seals, emblems, and trappings of the High Kingdom were to be destroyed.

The next day, Queen Angélique, the Kings, the questers, and the prisoners from Reingard used the portal to travel to Alesia, where Thor waited for them. The last to enter the portal was the Portal Keeper, and the portal closed behind him.

# CHAPTER 14

Deciding how the Eight Realms would work together was one thing. Creating a formal document that explained it in detail—which the rulers of the Eight Realms and the Grand Master would all sign—was something else entirely.

Thor had faithfully documented all of the decisions made the last time the Kings, Angélique, and the Portal Keepers had met, but when the Kings saw everything in writing, formalizing each detail, they balked at signing it. It took days of discussion, going through each section of the document in detail, before the Kings and Angélique would agree to the provisions of the document.

There were some changes made, but the core of the document remained largely intact, including a provision that Thor insisted upon which prohibited moving armies through the portals without the permission of the Grand Master, and then only to assist with a natural disaster or to come to the aid of a realm who had requested it.

Angélique was the first to sign her name to the document, which not only outlined how the realms would work together, but also reaffirmed the independence of the portals and the Brotherhood of Portal Keepers throughout the realms forever. Then each of the Kings signed the document. Thor signed it last, as Grand Master.

Thor's assistants made copies of the document for each of the Kings and Angélique to take with them at the end of the meeting. The original would remain in Alesia with the Grand Master, since he held the power to enforce the provisions through control of the portals.

"There is no more High Kingdom," Thor said after each realm's ruler received his or her copy of the document. "The Eight Realms of Annwyn are now independent realms who work together under the guidance of this council. The territories of Riverstone and Alesia remain independent from the Eight Realms, as does the Island of Dragons. As for the other islands around Annwyn, what happens to them will be decided by this council once they are explored and begin to have their own populations."

Thor's assistants brought in the prisoners taken from Reingard. "Now it is time to decide the fate of these prisoners. And before anyone suggests it," Thor said to the rulers, "there will be no executions. They will either be banished to another world chosen by the master portal, or they will be allowed to remain in Annwyn in one of the realms or territories."

Angélique stood. "There is no question of my sister Telise's guilt, and for her crimes I request that she be banished."

"Cowardly bitch!" Telise spat. "You haven't the

strength to deal with me yourself. You're pathetic."

"Don't judge her too hastily," Thor cautioned Telise. "I'm the reason you weren't hanged from your balcony. Your crimes committed here, namely your attempts to seize the portals for your own purposes, and the crimes you committed in Cockaigne through Viscount Ladrach, gives King Rigderg and me a say in what happens to you. That's why you're here and why you're not going to be executed. But I promise you, there are worse fates that await you on the worlds you might be sent to. Atreus, for instance, survived his exile for several days before he was foolish enough to enter the water. He was eaten by the carnivorous fish on that planet within minutes. Perhaps we can arrange for you to share his fate. He was your creature after all."

Telise began to tremble, but she said nothing.

Thor turned to King Rigderg. "Your thoughts, your Majesty?"

Rigderg stared at Telise. "If execution is off the table, then I say she should be banished. She is too dangerous to be allowed to remain on Annwyn."

"I agree," Thor said. Then he asked the other rulers, "Do any of you object?"

The Kings agreed to banishment.

"I further propose that Telise's councilors who are found guilty suffer her same fate," Angélique stated.

"I agree," Thor said.

The other rulers agreed.

Thor and the rulers then discussed the members of Telise's council. The Colonel who served as liaison between the council and the army was found innocent, but he was released from duty immediately.

The finance minister and the other ministers who

were stealing from the treasury were found guilty and sentenced to banishment.

Telise's slave master was found guilty, since slavery was outlawed everywhere on Annwyn, and he was sentenced to banishment.

Telise's spymaster was found guilty and sentenced to banishment.

All of the other ministers who helped devise and implement the tyranny that the High Kingdom had used against the realms over the years were also found guilty and sentenced to banishment. In all, thirty-five ministers and deputy ministers were being banished with Telise, while ten advisors and liaisons were being allowed to return to Reingard, but not in their former positions.

Thor then led the rulers of the realms and the prisoners to the portal, so their sentences could be carried out. He communed with the portal for a moment, and then he smiled. "You're all in luck. The portal has chosen your exile on the same world where the High Kingdom's former Portal Keeper was exiled for his collaboration with Telise. It's a lush world where you can live comfortably for many years, and you'll have each other's company. The former Portal Keeper can show you around."

Thor opened the portal, and the other world appeared on the other side. The former Portal Keeper could be seen nearby. "You're receiving company," Thor shouted to him. Then he ordered the prisoners through the portal to begin their exile.

Telise was the last to enter the portal. As her bonds were cut, she looked back at Thor and Angélique. "You'll never be rid of me. I'll get my revenge on both of you for this. Mark my words, this isn't the end."

Thor put his face close to Telise's and said, "The only revenge you'll get is in your dreams. There's no coming back from where you're going." With that, Thor pushed her through the portal and closed it after her.

Thor then looked at the other rulers. "Are you all ready to return to your realms?" he asked.

They nodded, and Thor opened the portal to their realms so they could go home. The Kings and the Portal Keepers left together.

When it was Angélique's turn to leave, she turned to Thor. "Thank you, Grand Master, for all you did for me, for Reingard, and for the realms." She gestured to the questers, who were standing nearby. "And thank you for sending these brave people to help me. I've learned more than I ever thought possible from them, and I will cherish our time together for as long as I live."

Thor bowed.

Angélique said goodbye to the questers, hugging each of them. Then she and Reingard's Portal Keeper entered the portal, and Thor closed the portal behind them.

"Can you stay for a while?" Thor asked the questers.

"For a day or so," Justin answered. The others nodded.

Thor looked at Ravana. "When do you want to return to Riverstone?"

"This afternoon, Grand Master. There are some records regarding those abandoned cities in the southern part of the territory that I'd like to look at first, if I may."

Thor smiled. "Of course. They have a fascinating history."

Thor led everyone back to the residence, where his assistants had lunch prepared. It was stew, which Nikki loved, and they enjoyed it thoroughly.

Shortly after Ravana had finished his research and was preparing to return to Riverstone, Allison asked him to step outside for a private conversation. No one could hear what was said, but Ravana had a curious look on his face when he and Thor headed for the portal a short while later.

"What was that about?" Bethany asked.

"I just needed to understand a couple of things about how the portal between Annwyn and Earth worked, particularly the part about what happens here staying here. I've been curious about it for ages, and since this will probably be my last trip here, I hoped to get some answers. Unfortunately, all I have is more questions."

"Is it something that Thor or I could answer?" Bethany asked.

"I don't think so." Allison didn't want to tell Bethany everything she had been talking about with Ravana, so she said, "One of my questions is what happens to a pregnancy if someone from Earth comes here, gets pregnant, and then goes back to Earth. Ravana didn't know, but he thinks it might end the pregnancy. So, you can't come back to earth until the baby is born."

Bethany nodded, and then her eyes opened wide. "Wait. You mean I *am* pregnant?"

"It's possible, but it's not very far along. You must have gotten pregnant the night you returned here after we rescued you. That was less than a month ago, Annwyn time, so most of the normal indicators haven't kicked in yet. But there are some early indicators that I *can* detect. You'll know for certain in the next few weeks, but be prepared, since this is your first pregnancy."

Bethany smiled. "I will. And if I am, and once it's born, I'll find a way to let you know."

"You'd better," Allison said.

They saw Thor coming back from the portal, and they waited for him before going inside and joining the others.

The questers stayed with Thor and Bethany for another day. They talked about old times and how their lives had changed ever since they began playing the game that had brought them all together. They stayed up all night, talking, laughing, and avoiding the inevitable.

When the sun began rising in the east, and the light streamed through the windows, the questers realized that it was time to say goodbye to Thor and Bethany.

"You know you're welcome to come back and visit any time you wish," Thor said as he hugged each of them. "I know you're not going to accept any more quests, but this is a unique place for the occasional vacation. Keep that in mind."

"We will," Nikki said.

Thor led them down to the portal, and he looked sad when he turned to face them again. "I hate goodbyes, as much as Bethany does, so I'll just say: Until we meet again."

"Until we meet again," the questers echoed.

Thor opened the portal to Riverstone, and the questers saw the tavern owner and his assistants waiting for them.

"Safe travels, my friends," Thor said.

Bethany nodded as tears streamed down her face.

"Have a great life, you two," Nikki said. Then she and Justin entered the portal, followed by the others.

When they reached the tavern, they looked back. Thor

and Bethany waved, and the questers waved back. Then the portal closed.

"Welcome back, courageous questers," Ravana said. "While I don't believe this will be the last time we see each other, I do believe that this was your last quest, and when we see each other again, it will be for pleasant reasons and not for perilous adventures."

The tavern owner sighed. "I shall miss sending you on quests. You were the best, and you quite literally saved this world. How often do you get to save a world where you live?"

"Not often at all," Justin confirmed.

Ravana nodded. "Now you get to return to your normal lives, but this entire world now gets to define a new normal—one that will govern us for centuries upon centuries to come. Thank you seems so... inadequate, but it's the best I have. On behalf of all of us, thank you."

Ravana hugged each of the questers, and when he reached Allison, he whispered something in her ear that no one else could hear.

Then the tavern owner looked at Nikki. "As far as your game controller is concerned..."

"I'll be disconnecting it when we get back home," Nikki confirmed.

"I understand. May I make a request?"

Nikki nodded. "Of course."

"Keep the game controller. Don't get rid of it. And use it every now and then to contact me here. I can keep you up to date on the news, and I can pass messages along to anyone you're trying to reach."

"I will," Nikki said.

Ravana smiled and put his arm on her shoulder. Then

he hugged her again.

As he pulled back, he asked, "Are you all ready to go home now?"

The questers nodded.

Ravana nodded, and he and his assistants moved behind the bar. He waved as the first crack of thunder sounded. Then the second crack of thunder was heard, coupled with the familiar flash of white light.

The tavern in Riverstone disappeared.

# The Final Journey Home

# CHAPTER 15

Nikki looked around at the inside of her living room. The tavern owner was on the TV screen, and everyone was standing exactly where they had been before they agreed to go on the quest... everyone except Allison.

Nikki looked around, and she saw Allison lying on the floor on the other side of the couch.

"Allison!" she cried, leaping over the back of the couch and checking on her unconscious friend. Allison didn't respond.

Nikki looked at the TV screen. "What happened?" she demanded. "Did the portal do this?"

The tavern owner looked confused. "We know that what happens here stays here, but I never thought that a resurrection could be undone the way injuries could be undone. Allison is the first person who has ever been resurrected by someone visiting from Earth. I had no idea how the portal would react, but I never expected this."

The other questers gathered around Allison, not knowing what to do.

"Can we send her back there with Livvy and try to resurrect her again?" Nikki implored.

"I don't know," the tavern owner said. "But if that works, Allison can never leave Annwyn again. You know that."

Nikki turned to Peter, who looked concerned. "I'll do whatever has to be done," he said. "Just bring her back to me."

Nikki looked at Livvy. "Will you go back long enough to resurrect her?"

Livvy, visibly shaken, nodded.

Nikki looked at the TV screen. "Bring Livvy, Allison, and Peter back there," she demanded.

"No," the tavern owner said.

"What?!" Nikki was enraged.

"No," the tavern owner said calmly. "There's no need for that."

Nikki wanted to throw something at the television, but she knew that Ravana would never feel it. Then she heard laughter. She looked around, but no one looked amused. They all looked as angry as Nikki felt. But the laughter continued.

The tavern owner was smiling, as were his assistants, but they weren't laughing. Then Nikki looked down at the floor.

Allison was laughing her ass off.

It took Nikki a minute to grasp what she was seeing. Then she dropped to her knees and grabbed Allison by the shoulders.

"What the hell is going on?" she demanded, shaking

Allison's shoulders.

The others stared at Allison with a mixture of shock and dismay.

Allison sat up and wiped the tears from her eyes. She stood, gave Peter a kiss, and waved to the tavern owner.

Nikki glared at Peter. "You were in on this?"

Peter shook his head. "I knew she was going to prank you when we got back, but I didn't know *this* was the prank she had in mind."

Livvy began slapping Allison's shoulder. "You bitch! I was scared to death. And this was just a prank? You fucking bitch!"

"I had to do it," Allison said.

"Explain," Justin demanded.

Allison stepped back so she could look at everyone at the same time. "Look, I'm grateful for what you did in Cockaigne by resurrecting me. But all of you have been looking at me strangely ever since. I get it. I was dead, and then I was alive, but do you have any idea how it made me feel to see all of you staring at me and treating me differently because of something that happened *to* me, rather than something I did? I couldn't take it anymore, but I didn't know how to make it stop. I finally decided that I had to do something radical to snap all of you out of whatever it is that scares you about me, and this is the best I could come up with. I told Peter why I was going to prank you, but not how. I needed his reaction to be genuine. Only Ravana knew the details, because I needed his help."

"And I readily agreed," the tavern owner said. "Allison was fully and completely restored when Livvy resurrected her in Cockaigne. You all needed to see that. Sometimes harsh measures are needed to bring about desired results.

Allison needs you to treat her normally, to see her normally, and this seemed as good a way as any to make that happen. I'm sorry if it scared you, but Allison didn't deserve to be treated the way you've been treating her any longer. You're home, you're safe, and she's the same person she was before you came here. You need to see her that way. I can assure you that she sees herself that way. If you're truly her friends, you will, too."

Nikki glared at Allison and then grabbed her and hugged her tightly. "I'm sorry, Allison. I've had people die around me before, but I've never had someone brought back from death before. I... I just didn't know how to process it."

"And I forgive you, Nikki, but I need you to get past it so we can be friends again. I need everything to be as it was before we left the last time. I can't stand being treated differently anymore."

Everyone stepped in for a group hug, and the others apologized to Allison, too.

Nikki looked at the tavern owner, who was wiping tears from his own eyes. "Well played, Ravana. Well played."

The tavern owner nodded. "Farewell, my friends. And don't forget to check in every now and then."

Nikki nodded. The TV screen went blank, and Nikki selected Game Over on the game console. Then she turned it off and unplugged it from the TV.

After she had wound the cords around the game controller, she looked at the others.

"So that was really our last quest?" Kevin asked.

Nikki nodded. "I think so. It was definitely my last quest."

"Mine, too," Justin said. "If any one of you wants my game controller, let me know. It's yours. Otherwise, Nikki and I will be keeping the two controllers in the closet from now on."

"I'm done with questing," Peter said, putting his arm around Allison's shoulder. "My wife and I have some seriously living to do here, and that's where I want to spend my time. I still want us to get together, but we need to find other things to do as a group that don't involve traveling halfway across the universe to battle evil."

The others laughed.

"I'll bet we can think of something," Livvy said. "Although, I have to admit, I'm going to miss the power of being a sorceress. It's quite a rush."

"I guess you'll have to get used to just being a chef, my business partner, and my wife," Kevin said, giving her a kiss on the cheek.

"It's a close second," Livvy said, "and I'll bet I can get used to it very easily."

After one more hug, Allison and Peter left, followed by Livvy and Kevin.

Nikki put the game console in the storage bedroom closet next to Justin's. Then she walked back to the living room and sat on the couch next to him.

"I need a vacation," she said as she put her head on his shoulder. "Something normal. Something of this world."

"I've been thinking the same thing. We've been running around Annwyn in the cold for weeks, and we've been surrounded by mountains and forests. I'm thinking beaches. Warm ocean water, sunlight, sand, and not a care in this world... or any other world for that matter."

Nikki saw her cell phone on the coffee table, and she

picked it up and looked at it. The time showed that it was six o'clock in the morning, but it was the same day they had left for Annwyn.

"We've been gone for two hours, earth time," she said. "I'll never get used to that... and I guess now I don't have to, since we're never doing that again. Just out of curiosity, which beach are you thinking about, and when are you thinking of going?"

Justin reached for his tablet, which was also on the coffee table where he had left it. He scrolled through the travel reservation site he used the most, and he asked, "Do you want to stay in the US, or do you want to go somewhere in the Caribbean?"

"Do you have a preference?" Nikki asked. "I've been to most of the beaches on the gulf coast, but I've never been to a Caribbean island before. The real question is: can we afford it?"

Justin entered some information into the tablet, looked at the results, and turned the tablet so Nikki could see it. "You tell me."

"Wow," Nikki said. "And that covers everything?"

Justin nodded. "It's off season, down there, but it's still warner there than it is here. If we go soon, we can more than afford it."

"Air travel included?"

"Air travel included," Justin confirmed.

"How quickly can we get this planned?"

"Two weeks?"

"Done."

Justin and Nikki had no trouble getting the time off work, and two weeks later, they were flying over the crystal blue waters off one of the more beautiful and romantic Caribbean island resorts.

As soon as they checked into their hotel room, they changed into their swimsuits and headed for the beach. Nikki had purchased her first bikini, having preferred one-piece swimsuits when she was in school and the army. It was blue-striped with a strapless bandeau top that was twisted in the center. She looked angelic in it, and Justin couldn't keep his eyes off of her.

As they played and swam in the ocean, Nikki put her arms around Justin's neck. "I want us to get married," she said.

"You do?" Justin asked.

Nikki nodded. "I've known it for a while. And not just because our friends are married or are getting married, but because I want to spend the rest of my life with you as more than just lovers. I want commitment. I want... I want it all, I guess. I can't put it into words, other than to say that *you* are what I want in this world... and in every other world we may or may not visit. I can't stand the thought of ever being separated from you again."

She looked deeply into his eyes. "Will you marry me and be mine like I'm yours?"

Justin smiled. "Did you know that I planned to propose to you on this trip?"

Nikki's eyes went wide. "Really?"

Justin nodded. "The ring's in the room. I put it in the safe while you were getting changed."

"So...?"

"Yes, I'll marry you. I never want to spend another day

without you, and I want us to be together for the rest of our lives. You complete me, and I'm no good without you. There is no one else in this world... in this universe... for me other than you."

Nikki kissed Justin as he wrapped his arms around her. When they separated, she said, "Why don't we go back to the room so you can show me that ring?"

"As long as that's the only thing you're wearing when I put it on your finger."

Nikki grinned. "I think I can agree to that."

They ran back to the room, stopping only to wash the sand off their legs with the outdoor showers around the pool. When they reached the room, Nikki removed her bikini and rinsed out the salt water before hanging it up to dry. Justin did the same with his swim trunks, and then he guided Nikki to the oversized shower in their bathroom.

They bathed quickly, and Nikki wrapped a towel around herself after she dried off. Justin did the same, and then he opened the safe and removed the jewelry box he had hidden there.

When he opened it, Nikki's face lit up. The ring was beautiful and exactly what she would have chosen for herself. She held out her hand so he could put it on her finger, but he shook his head.

"Remember our agreement," he said softly.

Nikki smiled and removed her towel.

In the diffused sunlight coming through the upper windows of the room, Justin looked at Nikki's body in awe of anyone or anything being so beautiful. He carefully removed the ring and placed it on her finger.

It fit perfectly.

She looked at it, and then she grabbed his towel and

removed it before wrapping her arms around his shoulders.

"I love it," she purred. "I love you."

"And I love you, Nichole," he whispered. "Thank you for wanting to be my wife."

"And thank you for wanting to be my husband."

"Nichole," Justin said softly, "do you remember what I told you the first time I was in your apartment?"

"Refresh my memory," she purred.

"I told you that, for me, love is a verb. It's what you do, not what you say. I may not say all the right things, but I swear I'll never stop showing you just how much I love you. I'll spend the rest of my life doing that as your husband."

She smiled. "And I swear to spend every day for the rest of my life proving it to you as your wife."

She reached up and kissed him. "I need you inside of me," she said softly in his ear.

He picked her up and carried her to the bed. With one hand holding her, he yanked the covers back and gently set her down. He laid down next to her, and she immediately spun around on top of him—facing away from him—so they could please each other at the same time. Both moaned as they stimulated each other's pleasure centers.

Nikki wanted to keep going as they were, but she needed to feel him deep inside of her. She spun around, facing him, and guided him inside, riding him as if her life depended on it.

They made love for the rest of the afternoon, and when they were exhausted, and famished, there wasn't a chair, desk, table, or wall that they hadn't used to satisfy their sexual needs.

They still wanted more, but they knew it would have to

wait until they had regained their strength. After a short rest, they showered again and went to dinner in the resort's main restaurant.

Nikki wore a flowery print dress with a single shoulder strap that wrapped around her waist and stopped well above her knees. Her engagement ring was the only jewelry she wore. Justin wore slacks and a button-up shirt, untucked.

After dinner, they walked hand-in-hand in the moonlight along the beach, watching the water glow as it crashed against the shore. This was paradise, and everything about it made them appreciate what they were sharing and what they were going to keep sharing together for the rest of their lives.

They returned to their room and fell asleep quickly. The next morning, after room service brought them a light breakfast, they put their swimsuits on and headed for the beach.

Once they were in the water, Justin realized that there was something about Nikki's bikini that made it impossible for him to keep his hands off of her.

They moved out away from shore, and Justin reached down the front of her bikini and began stimulating her clit. Nikki, grinning, reached down and began rubbing his erection, which was already quite large. Nikki climaxed several times. Twice, she had to put her head underwater so she could scream from the pleasure.

When Justin finally released, they headed back to shore and then to their room. They spent the rest of the day making love to each other. No matter how many times they made love, it never seemed to be enough. They wanted more, and they never wanted it to end.

On their last day at the resort, they decided to work on their tans, so their friends wouldn't think they had spent the entire trip in the bedroom. Justin's tan made him look even more rugged than before, and Nikki's tan made her skin glow even more, which made it harder for Justin to keep his hands off of her.

The next morning, the resort's shuttle took them to the airport for the return home. Nikki wore shorts and a t-shirt, and Justin had to close his eyes to keep from wanting to make love to her on the airplane. No one had ever distracted him like Nikki did—not just physically, but in every way possible. She had become his whole world, and he wanted to spend the rest of his life making her happy, just as she did for him.

The weekend after Nikki and Justin returned from the islands, the questers met for dinner at Livvy's restaurant. They sat at their usual table, and everyone got a good look at Nikki's engagement ring.

"Congratulations, you two," Livvy said when she saw the ring. "It's about time he asked you."

"Actually, Nikki asked me," Justin pointed out.

"But he was going to ask me," Nikki added, "and he had the ring with him in the room. I just asked first."

Allison put her hands over her heart. "That's so romantic. I love it!"

Kevin looked at Justin and grinned. "I'm surprised you found time to get a tan while you were down there."

"It wasn't easy," Justin admitted. "There were so many... distractions keeping us inside."

"Yeah, my bikini, for one thing," Nikki said, squeezing Justin's leg.

Justin nodded in agreement.

"That must have been some bikini," Peter said.

"It's not what you think," Justin said. "It's just... there's something about the way Nikki looked wearing it. I can't describe it, but it drove me crazy."

"So I bought four more exactly like it so I'll always have one handy when I need to drive him a little crazy," Nikki admitted. "You know... in case I can't find another one like it in the future."

Over dinner, Livvy and Kevin talked about their plans for the future, and Allison and Peter talked about what they'd been doing since returning home. It all seemed so blissfully normal.

It was Nikki who brought up quests. "You know, I was a soldier for many years, and I thought I had seen it all. Then we started questing, and I *really* thought I had seen it all. But now that soldiering and questing is behind me, I realize that having a normal life with Justin is the only adventure I need, and the only one I want for the rest of my life. Having friends like you, working with my uncles and cousins, working with Justin, and just being... *here*... it's all I need. It's all I'll ever need."

Justin squeezed her hand. "Me, too."

The other questers agreed.

After dinner, Nikki and Justin walked hand-in-hand back to Justin's car.

"You know, ever since Allison's prank, I've never once thought about what happened to her until this moment," Nikki said.

Justin looked at her. "I haven't either. I guess her

prank worked."

"Just as well," Nikki said. "Now that we're back to stay, I'm happy leaving all that in the past."

"Except for one part," Justin said.

Nikki stopped. "What part is that?"

"The part where we found each other."

"And the part where you helped me get over what happened to me in the army," Nikki reminded him.

"So, we remember the good things that brought us closer together, and we let the rest of it fade?"

Nikki nodded. "Absolutely. You're the only memories I need. As long as I have those, I have everything."

Justin smiled. "I love you, Nichole."

"I love you, Justin. From one end of the universe to the other, and from now until the end of time."

The End

# ABOUT THE AUTHOR

W. B. Speir is an Award-winning author. Born in Alabama, W. B. has lived in Michigan, Connecticut, Florida, and now resides in Texas. W. B. has 26 published novels, six of which are Royal Palm Literary Award Gold and Silver winners. W. B.'s novels span the Romance, Fantasy, Historical Fiction, Science Fiction, Espionage, Suspense, and Action-Adventure genres. *The Quester Trilogy* is W. B.'s first Romantasy series.

For more information about W. B., please visit the publisher's website at progressiverisingphoenix.com.

*If you enjoyed reading this book, please review it on Amazon, B & N, or Goodreads. Thank you in advance!*

Printed in August 2024
by Rotomail Italia S.p.A., Vignate (MI) - Italy